PROMISED

PROMISED GARDEN

A Garden Trilogy Novel

SABINA GRIGGS

authorHOUSE®

AuthorHouse™ LLC
1663 Liberty Drive
Bloomington, IN 47403
www.authorhouse.com
Phone: 1-800-839-8640

Published by AuthorHouse 04/07/2014

ISBN: 978-1-4969-0320-4 (sc)
ISBN: 978-1-4969-0319-8 (hc)
ISBN: 978-1-4969-0318-1 (e)

Library of Congress Control Number: 2014906532

IN LOVING MEMORY
JENNIFER RENEE PARISI

When a person is lost and drowning

in the search for themselves

They find answers in places nobody thinks to look

With people you never should have found

And the adventure of discovery is

astonishing and powerful

Find Yourself!

CHAPTER 1
ESCAPE

I hate riding the bus! Unfortunately I had to get a job to ensure that I had food and a way out in a few weeks when I turn eighteen. I would have rather stayed at work. I ended up extremely lucky. I got a job at a little nursery on the cusp of the ghetto. Close enough to home that I could get there, but far enough away that it was still nice. It wasn't run down or falling apart. It was even a pleasant color. I spent my day taking care of the plants. I seem to have a way with plants and animals. My boss says I have a gift, I think it just means I don't have a life. It has always made me happy to be around nature. I get nature better than people. Maybe that's because plants don't usually try to hurt you or drag you down for no apparent reason. Animals too, they are simple. Their reactions are based off of needs—Food, air, and water.

The only thing I have to do on this ride is people watch. Most of these people are just a product of unfortunate circumstances, like me. I can only feel a little bad for them. If they really wanted out they would find a way. Instead, they turn to the same things that put them here: drugs, gangs, alcohol, prostitution and poverty.

I am the exception to the rule around here. I am the outcast, even though my father is just like everyone else. I have a job, do my school work, and I even get good grades. I am going to get out of here. To everyone else it makes me a snob. I am too good for them. Well that isn't exactly the case; if they chose to be, they could be better. I think people have devolved, we no longer push ourselves to the limit to achieve our higher purposes; we take the easy road.

My stop lets off a few blocks away from my house, so I have to walk a bit. I try not to draw attention to myself. It's about dusk, so the actual bad people in this area start to come out. The ones who cause the unfortunate circumstances and are not just a product of them come crawling out of the cracks in the cement like cockroaches. If I'm not careful I will be forcefully recruited into something. One of the pimps was eyeing me with a sick hopeful look in his eye, probably hoping to enslave another employee. I tried to keep my pace steady but my breathing started to accelerate. I would not be trapped. I have survived in one piece for this long; I will not miss my opportunity to escape by three weeks. The walk always seems to take a very long time. It is probably just the anxiety.

I finally got to my house.

My house is a shabby looking one story building. It was provided by government funding. It used to be blue once upon a time but now it's faded, like everything else in this part of town, to a sickly looking grey. The faded paint is chipped and peeled. The window frames and the doors are damaged giving the house a disgruntled look. It almost looks alive. Like a hungry, angry monster. It gives me the creeps. I tried to grow a garden to give the place a cheerier look. Unfortunately, the soil here is as tainted as the people. The house devoured my flowers along with any hope there was of grass or healthy trees.

I thought I saw something out of the corner of my eye. I spun, panicked, ready for a struggle. My mind started racing faster than I could spin a round, *what if the pimp followed me!!!!*

When I made a complete circle I realized there was nobody there. It was just another one of the reasons I had to leave. I saw things out of the corner of my eye all the time; it has to be the stress of living in this area.

I checked the mail first . . . . there is a letter for me from San Diego State University. It was too late in the year for an acceptance? I opened the envelope and pulled out the folded piece of paper.

Dear Miss Stainy,

We are pleased to announce that a slot has recently opened up. We would be delighted for you to enroll with us. We are aware that it is so late in the year so if you have already accepted another school we understand. Please contact our administrative offices with your decision as soon as possible. We do not want to miss the opportunity presented here.

It was signed and there was a contact phone number under the signature.

OH MY GOD! Could this really be happening? I was prepared to take classes' downtown at the community college in a better neighborhood but this . . . . sunny southern California? Can it really be! I ran in the house and yanked the phone off the dock. I dialed the number; it rang once, and then put me on hold. I hated the stupid elevator music they played, it made me more anxious and the tune got stuck in my head. Could they be on the phone with someone taking my spot . . . . I hoped not, then finally a friendly female voice answered,

"San Diego State Admission, This is Emily how may I help you?" My excitement peeked as soon as I heard a voice on the other end.

"Hello, my name is Jenelle Stainy, I received a letter offering me a spot in enrollment for next year and would like to accept" It rushed out so fast I hoped she caught it all.

"Hold on just a second Miss Stainy, let me look it up for you." She said. I held my breath while I waited. After a couple of minutes I started to worry. Should it take her this long to find it? Is there something wrong? Was this letter a mistake? My angst was unnecessary. "Here we are, the slot is still available, and you said you wanted to accept?" she said still maintaining a professional, cheerful voice.

"Yes, very much so, thank you." I almost yelled it into the phone.

"All right then dear we will send you the forms you need for the financial department and your class schedule." She replied with laughter in her voice.

"Thank you so much, you just made my day." It felt like I was floating. This excitement was an exhilarating high.

"You're welcome and welcome to San Diego State." She said as her parting line before she hung up.

I spent the rest of my daily routine skipping through the house, whistling the irritating elevator music but too keyed up to get annoyed that it was still stuck in my head. I crossed the date out on the calendar feeling that much giddier. Only three weeks and now I have a farther escape. I cleaned up the house and started dinner.

After I was done eating I put the rest of dinner in the microwave, he knew where to find it if he came home. My life has become a crappy routine. I went into my room, laid on my crappy twin bed and stared at the ceiling.

While laying there I started fantasizing about the new path that my life was playing out. I should think about getting a tan before I move to southern California. I wonder how hard it will be to find a job. My scholarships cover living expense but that really doesn't include food and clothes. Then I will need to look into transportation. I'm sure they have buses but trying to work a work schedule around both school and bus schedules will be a pain. Other than those minor problems the life I could have could be amazing. Spending time on the beach, finding tide pools or other areas teeming with life will be close to perfection. The area will be ideal for me. If I can get a car it will be even better, then I will be able to travel to see the wonders of southern California.

I think I must have fallen asleep somewhere in my planning and fantasizing.

My father came home drunk with the most atrocious woman yet. She was sickly looking, apparently on drugs. Where did he find these women? He had been gone for a few days, almost a week, and so I was expecting he would need something. I was hoping it would be short; that I could tell him whatever lie would make him leave me alone without starting a fight. I didn't want to ruin my good mood.

"JEN!" My father screamed as he walked in the door. He still called me that, my mom used to call me that, but I feel he had lost his right to use any sort of affectionate nickname. And I couldn't stop thinking it as an affectionate nickname because of my mother.

"I'm right here; jeez there is no need to scream." I replied. I didn't show him any affection, and I never showed respect. Respect is to be earned. "Our house is so small you can't even call it a house, I can hear you on the other side, even if you use a normal voice."

"Aren't you rude!" the sleazy woman with him stated about the same time my joke of a father said "Watch your mouth!"

"I was just stating a fact!" I retorted to both of them.

My father ignored me that time and went on to the point he called me for "Jen, this is Tiffany," He gestured to the woman "We have spent the last few day together." He looked like he wanted some kind of response; I was hoping he knew better than to look for enthusiasm.

"And?" that's all he was getting from me.

"And," he looked irritated, good "we have decided we are in love."

I snorted, was he serious.

"Listen here young lady; Tiffany and I are going to get married. I think you need a woman in your life, maybe then you won't be so bitter. Plus, it's been almost ten years since your mom passed and soon you are going to be leaving home. You are almost an adult and you keep blabbing about college or some crap. I need someone here with me." I tried to listen to the rest of his nonsense. I was torn between anger and amusement. Did he think this was a funny joke? Was he really trying to make this about me? Like he actually cared about me or this woman?

"Hiya, hun" the feeble woman said "I am ready to be your new mom, come give me a hug" she extended her arms.

Amusement won over anger momentarily. I started laughing so hard it was hard to speak "You think . . . . you can be . . . . a mom?" another rupture of laughter made it hard to breathe. I tried to pull myself together but doing this let the anger seep through. "Have you lost your mind, first of all I am almost eighteen I don't need a woman in my life, I just need to get a life that doesn't involve taking care of my drunk, drug addict, joke for a father." The woman still had her arms extended. Apparently I didn't make myself clear enough. "You obviously can't take care of yourself, let alone someone else. For your sake, and any child's, I hope you can't have kids. Maybe the drugs have ruined your body, because they have obviously made you lose your mind!" She finally let her arms drop. On the surface she looked angry but I could see it in the way her eyes dropped that I had hurt her feelings. For some reason I didn't understand I almost felt bad for her. So I added "If you really want the chance to have a family, clean yourself up and start looking for a better partner than this." I gestured toward my father. "Otherwise you are no better than the rest of the trash here." I said as gently as possible. She looked at me, then at my father.

"Humph!" was her only response. Then she jerked her head so her nose was in the air. Apparently she made her decision, well then there is no need to feel sorry for her.

I turned my attention to my father. "As for you," he glared at me when I addressed him. "Don't you dare try to make this in any way about me! You don't care about me other than how it benefits you. The second I walk out that door you lose *all* of your government assistance so now you think you can use this" I gestured to the both of them "as your next means of support." The more I talked, the madder I got but I couldn't stop myself. "Second, of all the trash you have brought home you think this sorry excuse of a person is suitable to be a wife, let alone a mother," I could see they were both getting mad but I really couldn't care less, the truth hurts. I was too mad to consider any consequences my actions might hold "and I am not bitter because I don't have a woman in my life you idiot, I am pissed off because I am stuck with you as a miserable excuse for a father and the rest of my family wont come see me because you are horrible. I have never even met anyone from mom's side of the family. Your family is either dead, in jail, or just as bad as you are. And even if I couldn't get into college I was leaving your house because I can't stand you. I am only here because technically the law states I have to be. But fortunately for me I got accepted into San Diego State University today so now, not only am I leaving, I will be far enough away that you cant even try to drag me back into this miserable life." By the time I was done I was so mad I was trembling.

"You ungrateful brat" he said "How dare you speak to me like that. I am your father and you will respect me. You will also show respect to your new mother. We will be married in the morning and you will treat her like she belongs here. And big deal you got accepted into a university, how do you think you are going to pay for that? Do you think living is free? Especially in a big city!"

"HA! I don't respect either of you. If you want to get married, fine, that's your business but that thing will never be my mom. And how dare you try to compare her to my mother. She was the most beautiful, amazing, talented woman I had ever met. You never deserved my mother. And for your information I received a scholarship almost eight months ago. Apparently I am the first person to qualify for almost a decade." I was so mad I could hit them both.

"NOW LISTEN HERE JENELLE!!!" He screamed "AS LONG AS YOU LIVE IN MY HOUSE YOU WILL FOLLOW MY RULES, TIFFANY BELONGS HERE WITH ME AND YOU WILL TREAT HER LIKE PART OF THE FAMILY!" I automatically took a step back. I still really didn't want to get into a fight.

The look he got in his eye made me have an epiphany. I couldn't do this anymore, three weeks was too long to wait to turn eighteen. "You know what, your right; Tiffany does belong here with you." I admitted. And in truth she did. Even when I calmly told her to clean herself up and do better, she chose this life.

He looked pleased, and so did she, well that wasn't going to last. "I'm going to my room."

"Sure thing, hun" Tiffany said before my father could say anything. "I can understand you need a minute to take in the good news, right?"

"Sure" I responded, thick with sarcasm. How thick can you be? After everything I said, she seemed like she believed the impossible words that came out of her mouth. I guess she was completely delusional.

I went into my room to get my essentials. I grabbed me duffle bag from the bottom of my closet. I put in a few clean clothes, the pictures of my mom, a small fleece blanket, and my little jewelry box. I looked for my toolbox of sorts. It was more like a small bag that had my Swiss army knife, duct tape, a screw driver multi tool, and a flash light. I went into the bathroom to get my essentials. I put all my bathroom stuff in a small bag and put it and my tool bag in the pack. I went to get my purse to make sure I had what I needed. It had my wallet with all the money had saved up from the house funds that nobody knew about. It also had my driver's license (which was almost pointless since we didn't have a car) and my bus pass. In my purse I also had mace, lotion, and a few other random items. Alright I was ready to go. How sad, this was all I needed to leave home.

As I walked back to the front of the house with my bag and purse my father looked at me crudely, "Where do you think you are going?" He asked with a smug attitude.

I have to try to keep this as short as possible before I lose my short window of opportunity. "I am leaving, you two may belong in this house but I don't. Apparently this is where the trash of the earth belongs and I refuse to be a part of that, so I am gone." I started to walk towards the door, but he sidestepped and blocked my path. Usually he wasn't this coordinated when he was drunk, so he must just be high tonight.

"Where would you go? Do you think anywhere is going to take you in? You wont last a minute, and if you walk out that door, don't even think about coming back." He had an evil smirk like he thought this was going to stop me. "So why don't you just stop while your ahead, go unpack your bags, and make us something to eat." HA! He was so dumb if he thought he could control me, like his words were more than just empty threats.

"I would rather sleep in the park before I came back here. I will figure something out. Anything has to be better than being stuck here with you! Enjoy your life!" And that was my parting line. I walked out the door and hid. I knew I couldn't go in any sort of straight path to get free, just in case he decided to use force to get me back in the house. I also couldn't use the alleys. If I planned to keep my freedom I couldn't risk being attacked and forced into the horrible life the people here had. I had a secret place next to the house I used to hide when he got too drunk. If he didn't have a woman for a distraction he liked to use me as a boxing partner only I was more a punching bag than a partner. I think it used to be a cellar or something but it was the same faded grey looking color as everything else so it blended in. It couldn't have been very long, maybe fifteen minutes but it felt like hours waiting, listening to the strenuous silence in the house. Finally, two cop cars pulled up in front of the house. Apparently he called the police to report me as a run away. After the cops showed up I listened harder, I could hear them in the house if I was quiet and listened hard.

My father met them at the door, acting like a concerned parent. He invited them in.

One of the officers spoke first "So what exactly is the problem here sir?"

"My daughter is gone!" I had to concentrate on my temper for a minute, I was grinding my teeth, and my face felt hot. How dare he refer to me as his daughter! I am a victim and he is my predator, not me his child and him my parent.

Apparently I missed something while I was focusing on my temper because when I tuned back in my father was no longer pretending. He sounded aggravated.

"She is a run away, go get her and bring her back." My father said.

"I need a description to find her." The officer replied using a professional voice "It will be easier if I can get height, weight, hair color, eye color, what she was wearing, and age. This form will give all that information if you can fill it out."

It was quiet for a few minutes so I guessed he was filling it out. Then, I could hear him and Tiffany in the other room. He must be at the kitchen table, I wonder if the cop could hear them too. "When she comes back I am going to give that child a beating like she has never had before" he was telling her. "I may even get lucky; we could get some serious money if she becomes permanently disabled, as long as she can't talk."

"Don't hurt her too bad babe, you don't want to get in trouble ya know" She replied. How horrible for them to say things like that with a cop in the living room. It was bad enough they were discussing my demise in the process of finding me but to do it with the repercussion in the other room was just ignorance. I heard the cop call for back up; good he must have heard them too.

"All right officer, got it all filled out." My father said as he walked back in the room. I'm assuming he gave the form to the officer. I guess the cop decided to read the form out loud.

"Five-seven, hundred and fifteen pounds, dark red hair, green eyes, was wearing jeans and T-shirt, birth date is May twenty-fifth . . . . Sir, today is the fourth of May, according to this your daughter is almost eighteen?" The cop asked.

"Yea but she has three weeks" My father exclaimed.

"Sir," The cop sounded amused "we can't do anything about this."

"What the hell do you mean you can't do anything about this, send out some cops and find her and bring her back!" He was starting to raise his voice, wow, he was dumb.

"Now sir, there is no need to raise your voice at me" the cop sounded irritated "I just cant afford to dispatch my officers for an almost adult who left home, we have more serious things to take care of. Even if I did try I could only afford to dispatch one officer and by the time he found her she would probably be an adult."

"So what am I supposed to do, just let her go?" He was still giving the cop an attitude.

"I will keep an eye out for her in case she needs help with anything. Do you know if she has any problems with drugs or gangs?" The cop asked. I couldn't get mad that he asked about that. In this part of town kids started into that by the time they were in middle school if not younger.

"No," my father had a weird emotion in his voice. I couldn't tell if he was offended or amused. It sounded like a mixture of both almost. He answered the cop a little more in depth "she is too much of a snob for any of that. She even put herself in independent study because she was too good for the people at the school." And then he added "Is that it then?"

"As far as your daughter is concerned yes, sir there is nothing we can do."

My father started to grumble, he started to say "Well then if you don't mind . . . ."

The cop interrupted him before he could finish his sentence "However, I need to ask you a few more questions . . . ." The cop sounded amused again "I will need you both to come down to the station with me." About that time three more officers showed up. "Sir, I am placing you both under arrest for suspicion of drug abuse as well as participation of other criminal activity" He stated.

"Under arrest?" He sounded stunned "We don't abuse drugs, and what other criminal activity? I have a right to know exactly what you think you are arresting me for."

"Well, due to the conversation you had in the other room, I am pressing charges for intent of assault and fraudulently claiming government assistance. Those are the charges I can claim so far." the officer explained.

I heard a small commotion that I assumed meant he tried to run. It sounded like him hitting the floor, and there was a smaller thud which I assumed was her hitting the wall. I also heard him spout a few swears and threats, which was only making his case worse.

Eventually the cops won. I watched from a small crack in the door of my hiding spot as they both were carted out in hand cuffs. My fathers lip was busted and his eye was starting to swell. Tiffany didn't look as bad as he did. Her hair was a little more ruffled then before and it looked like her shirt was ripped but other than that there didn't seem to be any change in her physical appearance.

I had to wait a while for the cops to search the house and find all the evidence they needed. From the sound of it, both of them were going to be in jail for a long time. When they all finally left I made my escape. I cut through the alley went up a few streets. I tried to make it fast. I really didn't want to run into anyone. I finally made it to my destination, the bus stop. I had to wait a little bit, which made me nervous. Finally the bus came, I showed my bus pass and the driver greeted me politely, eyeing my bag, but made no comment about how late I was riding or where I was heading. As I took a seat in the back of the bus I finally started to relaxed. I had done it, I escaped, and for the first time I didn't know what to expect tomorrow.

There was only one other person on the bus wearing a green hooded shirt. This person kept their hood up and was hunched down so I assumed the person was asleep. They didn't seem threatening in any way. Whoever it was was small in both height and width so I decided to ignore their presence. Freedom is very relaxing; I rested my head on the back of the seat and closed my eyes.

CHAPTER 2

WAKING UP

I could feel consciousness coming. It always made me sad to wake up. Another day meant more hell. My father was probably passed out drunk with whatever woman he had the night before. Which meant I had to clean the house up before I started my schoolwork? Fortunately my father agreed to let me do independent study so I would be home more often, outside of work. Unfortunately, I don't have any friends to ease some of my miserable day. Nobody wants to spend time with the local outcast. The dream I had I finally left my father's house, before I slipped into a black dreamless sleep, I didn't want to wake up from it. My fantasy world was much more pleasant. Somewhere in my fretting I realized that it didn't feel like I was lying on my bed. My bed was small and lumpy. Did I fall asleep outside? No, it felt like I was lying on grass but smelled like flowers. We didn't have much of either around my shabby little house.

Maybe I was still dreaming.

I slowly opened my eyes and gasped. I had never seen anything so beautiful, even in my imagination. My pallet was a bed made out of leaves and flower petals. I was covered by the most beautiful willow tree I have ever seen. Its branches swayed in the breeze but still completely obscured the rest of my surroundings like a curtain. I had no idea where or what this place was but I felt secure. It's strange that I didn't even feel this at home. The last time I had this feeling was before my mom died. That was almost ten years ago.

I decided to see what was outside my shelter, maybe this was a real place and I could recognize my surroundings. I got up and walked slowly to the edge of my little shelter. I shifted the willow branches slightly to peek through. *Oh my!* How could such a place exist, this had to be a dream, no place like this could be real. How unfortunate, but I knew it was time to wake up. I could not let this wonderful dream continue or my day may be that much harder to bear. So I went to lie back down. Going to sleep in my dreams usually woke me up.

How odd? Why isn't this working? Maybe . . . . I could only hope, but maybe . . . . this isn't a dream. How could I have ended up in such a beautiful place? I tried to remember the night before. Was what I thought a dream real? Did I really leave my fathers house? If that were the case then the last thing I remember is the bus. I guess I could have fallen asleep on the bus but then the dream theory of this place makes more sense. Unless I didn't dream, or couldn't remember dreaming, but then how did I get here? Clearly this isn't on a bus route.

I got up again and stepped out of the willow curtain. I still couldn't believe my eyes. It appeared that I was in a forest, but not like any of the forests any where near where I lived. The trees varied from pine and oak to trees that I couldn't find a name for. They flowed harmoniously together, even though they were so mismatched, they seemed to belong. In the distance I could see what looked like a mountain climbing into the clouds.

Okay I need to think about it logically. Option one I was dreaming and my mind refused to wake up. This is highly possible and even highly probable. Option two, someone killed me in my sleep on the bus or before I even got on the bus and this was heaven. The killing part was extremely possible but I would have remembered *something*, wouldn't I? Option three this place was real. If option three is true which seems unlikely, but if, then how did I get here and why am I here? I can only hope this place is real but can't seem to shake this gut feeling that I am missing something. There has to be a negative. Nothing comes without a price.

Then I heard something . . . . it sounded like . . . whispering? I looked around but couldn't see anyone. I started to walk, trying to make a mental map of my surroundings so I could find my way back to the willow tree if necessary. Everything was lush and beyond belief. The trees were huge and the leaves were a brilliant deep green, I couldn't find a single brown spot on any of them and no dead branches. The grass was soft and full, it reminded me of shag carpet. There were flowers everywhere: on the trees, in the grass, and bushes. The sky was clear with wispy clouds that looked like white smoke. And the air . . . had a taste impossible to describe . . . . it was warm and breezy and smelled like flowers and—happiness, it's just perfect.

As I walked I heard water. It sounded close so I followed a small footpath. I found a small running stream. The water was so clear that if it wasn't moving and reflecting light I wouldn't be able to see it. It flowed into a large pond with a natural spring running from a short cliff. In the cliff looked like a cavern opening. It was an awe inspiring sight that nearly knocked the breath out of me.

As I stood there dumb founded I heard a new sound. It was hoofs ruffling in the grass. As I watched a large horse immerged from the trees to drink from the pond. I was still a little ways away but I could see the rear end of the magnificent white horse as it bent its head to get a drink. I could hear the water splashing. I gasped. The horse heard the sound and turned in my direction.

As soon as I was able to see the horse head full on I knew I must be either dreaming or dead. This was no ordinary horse, it was a unicorn. The beautiful gold tinted horn protruding from the center of his head glistened in the sun. It stared at me like it knew something I didn't, the look in the unicorn's eye looked like a strange mix of recognition and relief, and it was unsettling.

Again I heard whispering, and this time it was accompanied by . . . . giggling? It sounded like a small tinkling bell but had the same rhythm as a giggle.

"Who's there?" I called trying to sound firm, even though I was fairly certain this wasn't real, I was still nervous to have someone following me that I couldn't see.

"Shhhhh!" I heard someone say.

"I can hear you! Show yourself!" I said again, hoping to figure out what was going on, and also maintaining a brave façade.

Then a woman who was barely clothed walked out from behind a tree. Her clothes looked like a combination of leaves and flowers; it didn't look like it could be considered more than a slip. Her face and body seemed to be beyond beautiful. I have never seen this degree of beauty, even on the cover of fashion magazines. Her hair was deep brown but seemed to have a strange green tint to it, almost like her hair was grass stained. Her eyes were the same color green as the leaves around her. She was tall and thin but still had a full figure most girls would kill for. Her skin was a very light color but had the same green tint that her hair did. Maybe the sun was reflecting through the trees? But she was standing in the deepest part of the shade.

"Hello." The woman said in a voice so pure, but also so strong and confidant it momentarily erased my sense of unease.

"Hi." I managed to choke out in my astonishment.

"My name is Arhea, you look very confused and a little frightened, I apologize for this but I did not think you would believe where I wanted to take you unless you saw for yourself. Please let me know at any point if it is no longer your wish to be here and I will deliver you safely back to where we retrieved you." She looked sincere and a little remorseful; her hands were outstretched in front of her like she wanted to comfort me.

"I'm sorry but you're right I'm confused. Where am I? Where did you find me? Why did you want to bring me here?" I asked my questions slightly rushed, without leaving a break for her to answer, but this just didn't make sense and was even less believable. She said she would take me back though, so hopefully that meant she didn't want to hurt me.

"This is my garden; I am very fond of things beautiful, talented, and rare. Most of the creatures and plants that can be found here are difficult to find and some are even considered fable." She replied.

"That doesn't really answer my questions, not all of them at least. I'm sorry if I'm being rude, I just really want to know what's going on. I mean, I think I just saw a unicorn for crying out loud and that can't be possible, can it?"

"That was Perilus. He is a close friend of mine. He is very special, even for a unicorn; He is king of the unicorns here, as a matter of fact. He is gifted even amongst his own kind. Most of the creatures here have their own fellowships. As for your questions, this garden lies on an island that cannot be found unless you are called or brought here. I found you sleeping on a bench outside of a strange building that seemed to house large vehicles, and I brought you here because I promised I would." When she finished her explanation she looked at me, waiting.

Okay so I was brought here, if here is real, and she said she found me at what I am assuming was a bus garage. If I was on a bench someone must have moved me, but why didn't they wake me up to get off the bus. And why didn't the fact that someone moved me wake me up.

"Other creatures? Okay, I'm not sure how things work here, wherever here is, but there are some serious holes in your story. Maybe you don't know what kind of neighborhood I come from but there is no way I would have slept through being moved once, let alone twice. And how can nobody find this island? We have satellites map the world and what promise are you talking about? Who did you promise? "I felt frustrated. I knew I should be grateful for being here but I couldn't shake the feeling that I was missing something and that this isn't all just rainbows, smiles and sunshine.

"Do not fret Jenelle; I had a close friend of mine keeping an eye on you. When your mother passed I promised her I would keep you safe. So I have and now that you freed yourself from your oppression I brought you here, however it is your choice to stay." she sounded so sincere I really wanted to trust her, but that just wasn't who I was.

"You know my name? You knew my mother? What friend? I didn't see anybody" I was stunned to hear this new information. I still tried to remember a person. There was the one person on the bus other than the bus driver.

"Your mother was born here, she left when she was about your age, and she wanted to see the outside world. She had heard stories but even though some of them were not pleasant she still wanted to see for herself. I had Alalia accompany her. Your mother fell in love and married your father. When she conceived you Alalia came back to share the news. We were intrigued to hear this news. Alalia kept tabs on your mother and you. When your mother got sick Alalia urged Amelinda to return so we could treat her, but she refused. She didn't want to leave your father or take you away from him but she couldn't leave you either." She explained.

"She left me anyway and I would have been better off without staying with my father." I mumbled mostly to myself. Of this story is true then she refused to get better. A mixture of anger and refreshed sadness caught in my chest.

"I know, you have my condolences, but Alalia stayed with you most of the time. She felt it was her duty. That's how I knew where to find you." She replied with remorse in her eyes and voice. It was almost as if she could see the pain in me.

"Who is Alalia? I never saw anyone there and I have never heard that name." I asked. I was still completely confused and the anger and sadness were turning my confusion to irritation, making my tone sharp.

"She was to remain hidden; we did not want to interfere with your life. It was in accordance with your mothers wishes. I shall introduce you to all in my garden in time but you must be hungry, why don't we go back to the great willow for some lunch." She said then she smiled.

"Okay, I guess I could eat first." I was still hesitant but I really didn't want to argue with her. The confusion was what was bugging me. I haven't found a reason to feel unsafe yet. If she wanted to hurt me or have someone else hurt me, then she would have when I was sleeping. Also my stomach was slightly rumbling.

As we walked, again I heard the whispering mixed with the strange tinkling giggle. I looked around but saw nothing. The only person with me was Arhea and she was completely silent as we walked. She just led the way and didn't look, so maybe she didn't hear it. Or I was crazy. I was also hearing more footsteps and hoofs rustling and leaves moving. It seemed like everyone here was following but staying hidden. But could there really be that many here? I tried to look closer when one of the leaves moved but by the time I looked all I saw was a pair of wings. Was it a bug? I hadn't seen any bugs since I woke up, not even near the water.

We got to the tree and she parted the leaves and held them for me to walk through. How did the setting change already? The bed of flowers was no longer there; in its place were a table and two chairs. The set looked like it was made out of the roots from the tree. As I thought about it, I didn't see metal anywhere, or houses. Where did everyone live?

Arhea gestured for me to take a seat. I did and she sat after I was seated. She sat there quietly. I waited for several minutes for her to say something but she just stared at me.

"What?" I asked. I couldn't understand why she just kept starring.

"You look very much like your mother." That was her response. I flushed a little feeling a little uncomfortable with her starring.

"Ummmm, so are we going to eat?" I asked after a few more minutes of silence, and her starring. I was trying to tone down my usually sarcasm and mistrust.

"Oh yes, I was lost in thought . . . . Darion?" I didn't see who she was speaking to. Well to be honest I couldn't see outside the tree at all.

"Yes ma'am" a light masculine voice answered. I couldn't see so I couldn't be sure but it sounded like a young voice. It didn't sound like he could even be close to a man his voice was so soft.

"Would you be a dear and get Jenelle and I something to eat and drink?" She asked to the still invisible boy.

"Coming right up ma'am" he replied

"He will be right in with lunch" she said turning back to me and starring again.

"So why was my mother here? You said you like things beautiful, talented and rare before, I know she was beautiful but what talents did you like of hers?" I asked to break the silence but also this was the first person, other than my father, who actually knew my mother.

"Well other than what she was, she had a gift for communicating. We used to call her our peacemaker because if any of the fellowship leaders had a problem with another person or persons they would come to her. She also did well in relationships both romantic and family. These were her most recognized gifts, but she had some that were under developed but promising" she explained.

"What she was?" I hadn't missed that she said *what* instead of *who* nor did I understand it really. Plus it sounded rude to say what . . . like she was property not a person.

24

As soon as I asked I was interrupted. A young boy came in carrying a tray, also made of wood, into the willow. Only he wasn't a boy. He was young, as I suspected, but the bottom half of his body looked like it was a goat and he had pointed ears and horns.

"Here we are" he said as he turned. Then he stopped and he was looking at me with an expression that I would assume matched mine. He recovered himself before I could.

"Hello there." He said to me. Again all I could do was stare. My dream theory was making more sense but I had no idea my imagination was so creative.

"Okay, we have passion fruit juice and I made some of my secret wraps." He smiled then and winked at Arhea. She looked at him with pleasure, like I was intruding on an inside joke.

"You know how I love those. Did you finish your studies?" She asked. It sounded like a normal question it just seemed out of place here.

"Yes I did, was there anything else you needed?" he responded

"No, no. You need to get back to your mother now. I am sure you have things you need to attend to there" She laughed.

"Alright, thank you, I will see you tomorrow." And then he left the space shielded by the willow branches.

I still hadn't been able to pull my expression together. I just sat there starring dumbfounded, mouth hanging open, trying to come to grips with what I just saw. First with this strange place, then the unicorn, Arhea knowing my mother, and now this! What kind of place was this? If by some miracle this place was real, how can such a thing be? I could only hope this was real but I still couldn't wrap my head around what I had just seen. Arhea noticed my expression and smiled at me.

"I know it is a lot to take in. I am trying to ease you into this world. I have not had experience in this form of education. I am sorry if this is moving too abruptly." She looked at me like she was waiting for something. I am not sure if it was a response or a reaction. I was still trying to pull myself together.

I finally decided that it didn't matter if this world was real or in my head. I needed to be prepared for what I was in the middle of so I figured it was best to get everything cleared up. I finally figured out how to pull my expression together about the same time I found my voice.

"I don't want to be eased into this too much, and I don't want anymore surprises like that. I'm sure I was very rude to your friend with my starring and not saying a word. So why don't you tell me what to expect so the next time I don't act quite like an idiot." I was probably a little more abrupt than necessary, and my attitude was a little harsh, but I was still in a little shock.

"As you wish, you have met Perilus the king of the unicorns so you know about them, and that was Darion, he is one of the youngest satyrs in my garden. I am a Hamadryad, I rule the nymphs here in my garden. There are centaurs and Pegasus as well as pixies, fairies, merfolk, and many other creatures, some that are not so pleasant. Only this half of the island is mine. The other belongs to Alysia, she is an Arachne. She is not fond of me but rarely do I have any interactions with her. If you wish to not be taken by surprise then your most advised course is to lose your preconceived notions of the world. As I stated earlier, most of the creatures here are considered fable. I think it will be better for you to slowly realize them instead of me listing them all." She finished.

"Okay, and this Alysia . . . um . . . . er . . . . person" I couldn't remember what she had called her "I am assuming she has the unpleasant creatures?" I asked

"Mostly" was her only response but she had an odd smirk when she said it "Now let us eat; there is much to do before I show you where you will be staying" she hesitated "That is if you wish to stay?" She amended.

It took me a moment to answer. There was so much that could be viewed as wrong with this. Finally I answered, "I suppose I can stay, at least for a little while, maybe for a couple of days." I really wanted to stay and believe this was real but I still had a feeling that I was missing something and/or this was a dream.

We ate in silence. The food was beyond amazing, I was starting to wonder if there could be anything wrong with this place. I tried not to let my hopes turn into beliefs. It would only be that much more crushing if this turned out to be a dream— or worse, a trick. I honestly don't know which would be more devastating.

When we were both finished, she sat and stared at me again. The look on her face was strangely hopeful. She didn't stare in a creepy way necessarily but it still made me uncomfortable.

"So what all do we have to do before you show me where I am sleeping?" I asked mostly to break the silence, but I was also curious, and strangely nervous. I guess I keep waiting for this to turn into a dream or something not so pleasant. It felt like waiting for the climax in a suspense movie.

"To answer that I guess I should explain to you about me first, so you understand." She smiled and looked at me with humor in her eyes before continuing with "It seems you get easily frustrated if you don't know the answers before you can ask the questions."

"Ok? What about you?" I tried to ignore the second comment. It was true but still a little frustrating and slightly embarrassing.

"I come from a long line of high ruling Hamadryads. So I was raised with a sense of regality. However, my family was humble even in power. So I learned a reverence for all life."

"That sounds like it would be a good thing." I said

"Yes, and as you learn the cycle in the garden, it should help you understand how and why things work here." she explained

I wasn't sure what to say. I really couldn't ask a question until later, when I knew what I was asking about. So after a moment of silence she continued.

"Other than ruling the nymphs here I am also, I guess you would call it a counsel leader, as well as the head of education and of course primary leader of the garden considering it does belong to me." She smiled at me, and then answered in more depth "So we have to have a counsel meeting to announce your arrival, then I need check the fields to ensure all is well. My teachings are done for the day so I believe that is all, unless something comes up along the way." She sort of rolled her eyes at that. The look kind of reminded me of a mother dealing with her children when they were misbehaving. "So I guess we should be on our way. Are you ready?" As she asked her expression turned into a mixture of reassurance and a warning.

"Yup, let's go." I tried to sound sure but my voice cracked. She smiled and held out her hand. I took it and again felt that strange sense of security I haven't felt since my mom died.

CHAPTER 3

MEETING

We left the willow on the other side this time. The woods here had a small break for what looked like a footpath. It wasn't warn in the sense that the grass or plant life was broken or dying but like the grass was a velvet carpet and the plants parted in a perfect line on either side. The path was covered by a flawless arch made by the trees. It felt like walking through a hall only the walls were structured from nature. It led to a clearing that had what looked like desks made of tree trunks and roots. There were several smaller desks that surrounded one larger one in a half circle formation that stood a few feet taller than the others. Arhea walked to the larger desk and took her seat. She gestured to the tree root seat next to her for me to sit.

As I took my seat she said "The others will join us shortly, just remember to rid your mind of any preconceived notions." After her reminder I heard hoofs against grass and leaves rustling. Perilus was the first through the trees. I recognized him almost immediately and even though I had seen him before I still had trouble wrapping my mind around the existence of unicorns. I tried to keep my face smooth and lock my expression that way. I was sure after Arhea's warning there were going to be more surprises and I really didn't want to make a fool out of myself.

Next into the clearing were two satyrs. One was male and he was frightening. The expression on his face was stern. The other was a woman, she looked uncomfortable when she first walked into the clearing and then her eyes met mine and she got the same odd expression Arhea wore when she stared at me. It was uncomfortable at the very least and confusing at best.

Again I heard that strange tinkling giggle, and someone shushed it just like the first time I had heard it. I looked over to the other end of the clearing and on top of one of the tables stood two very tiny people with wings. One was slightly larger than the other but judging but appearance I was assuming the smaller of the two was a child. She giggled again and the older of the two gave her a reproaching look. They wore simple but elegant clothing. The cloth was form fitting a looked like it should have been see through but somehow wasn't in most places. They were very pretty from what I could see and seemed to shimmer slightly.

Next I heard splashing; I looked around and noticed a very small pond at the end of a river. In the pond I saw the upper half of a man and a woman neither wearing a top. The woman's hair covered her chest and was an astonishing silver color. As I watched a tail splashed against the water. The procession continued. I tried not to act surprised when a man walked into the clearing with the bottom half of his body as a horse, or the Pegasus, but I couldn't help myself when a woman walked in who looked the most human yet. She was almost as beautiful as Arhea but she didn't have the green tint to her hair and skin. There were people with pointed ears that came in wearing clothes that looked similar to Arhea's but covered more of their body, and then there were several others with the same pointed ears. These were some of the most similar and diverse. Some were tall and thin, looking graceful in complete stillness;

others were short and stout looking as though they worked hard labor. It was hard to take in all of them as they surrounded where we sat, standing along the tree line, sitting at the desks, even some in the tree's. The last into the clearing looked similar to the small people on the table. They were a couple inches smaller and had a faint blue luminosity to their skin. Their ears were pointed and their wings were shaped differently. The most shocking thing was they were stark naked. They all settled in their various places, and all their attention was on Arhea, well mostly Arhea, they kept looking at me as well with a mixture of expressions that all confused me.

"Since most of us are here I shall begin. I already came with the assumption that a few of our friends would not attend, as they rarely do." She smiled and continued "For the first order I would like to introduce Jenelle" She gestured toward me "She will be staying with us until she decides to leave so I assume you will all make her feel welcome" With that she shot a look at the male satyr like she was directing this at him and his stern expression.

A few murmurs started but settled quickly. "For our second order, Nyx?" She turned to the bluish people. One of them turned her nose in the air "You have to stop tormenting the centaurs, Pegasus, and unicorns." She scolded "I do not want to have to put you on trial but will be forced to if you refuse to behave. I know it is in a pixies nature to steal horses but I do not allow you to live here to steal from me, nor are these true horses. You know how fond of you I am, please try to control yourself." She smiled at the pixie and Nyx softened and grinned back with pointed teeth.

"For my final order, please try to remember that I have sectioned off parts of the garden to protect some of our more private guests, please refrain from going there without having myself accompanying you." She said this like she was trying to protect everyone, she had a motherly tone to her voice. "Now is there anything that anyone would like to discuss?" She asked returning to her normal tone.

"I have a concern." The older of the two clothed winged people said. I assumed they were fairies.

"Yes, Caelia?" Arhea responded.

"In a short time I will be passing my crown to Sarette and as I try to take her with me to show her the duties and responsibilities of her birthright, some seem hesitant or even refuse to acknowledge her place. How do you suggest we go about resolving this?" Caelia asked.

Arhea first gave a look to Caelia then directed her attention back to the rest of the field "First I will suggest that all should treat the princess the same as you would the queen, second," She looked back at the fairy queen and said "Caelia, you must remember that your regal rights are only required acknowledgement within your own fellowship. You are the Queen of Fairies but not the queen of the garden. Please remember this and try to be a little more understanding. Each group of guests I have in my garden has their own form of leadership and is only doing as you wish your fairies to do."

The queen stuck her nose in the air and humphed. Apparently this wasn't the answer she was looking for. The rest of the group seemed to share the same smug smile. I guess this queen thinks she rules everyone. The fairy princess rolled her eyes at the queen.

Next one of the smaller men with pointed ears stood up. "I have a small matter I would like to discuss." He had a very gentle voice. He continued without waiting for any response "I know that you feel strongly about some of your more private guests but could you please try to make a visit and express the need to keep their abilities in their allotted area. I am sure I am not the only one who is tired of repairing their homes." He was firm but not rude.

Arhea looked like she was going to object but then her expression changed. "I will find time to stop by and see the ones you are referring to, as I am assuming it is Jarita and Kalian." Her expression turned apologetic "further more, I will do my best but we all know that these guests have formidable powers and I can only try to persuade them to control the range of their abilities."

The group seemed to get uneasy at this comment. I started to as well. Formidable gifts? Is this the part my gut instinct was warning me about from the beginning? I was starting to rethink how long I was actually going to stay here.

After the elves' request everyone seemed to be done. I was starting to feel the same way. I looked at Arhea and she first looked at me, and then turned to the group.

"If that is all for the day?" She waited a moment for anyone to object, no one did. "Well," she continued "Meeting adjourned. We shall meet again but I seem to have guests to attend to before I finish my business for the day." After she said her piece everyone slowly departed until it was just the two of us left in the clearing.

I sat there trying to absorb everything I saw and heard through this short but life altering meeting. Aside from myself and the one woman, there was nothing but mythical creatures; well I am sure there are more people from the woman's group but other than that. There were some I haven't seen yet, and some I am not sure if I want to see. Something about formidable gifts had my teeth on edge. This place was wonderful and magical but also strange and frightening. I am not sure why but part of me is trying to be logical and find reasons not to stay the rest of me doesn't ever want to leave. With each passing minute it felt like a magnetic pull was binding me here.

Arhea broke into my reverie, "Jenelle, I am going to leave you to attend to these guests." She informed me. "It's not that I do not trust you, but if you were afraid of being rude before; this would be an entirely different level of surprise even if I were to prepare you. With that, it would be unwise and dangerous for you to be rude in this specific company. Do you think you will be able to find your way back to the willow from here?" She asked

"Yes, am I able to look around on my way back, or do you want me to just go to the tree and wait?" I really didn't want to be left alone but couldn't help the relief that filled me. I think I might need a little more adjusting time before I tried to expose myself to the hidden guests and their formidable gifts.

"You may go where you wish Jenelle; you do not need to ask my permission. I do ask that you try not to stray too far though today. I need to be able to find you when I return so I can show you where you will be staying." She smiled a very fond smile at me "I shall return as soon as possible, do you need anything before I leave you?"

"Ummm . . . . " I didn't know how to word this without it sounding stupid, I guess stupid is what I get "I might need to use the bathroom while you are gone, is there somewhere for me to do that?" I felt odd asking a question that seemed tedious and normal in these surroundings, and I didn't need to go now but when nature calls you have to answer, so best to be prepared.

"We have facilities set, I will have someone check in on you after a while and if you need to, you can have them show you. Is that alright?"

"Yeah that's fine, other than that I am good. I guess I will see you in a little while."

"Yes" was her only response before she left in the other direction towards the mountains.

I started walking in the general direction of the willow tree, just not on the path. Everything here was so pretty, it reminded me of the stories about paradise before Adam and Eve were forced to leave. Again I couldn't be sure. I had only heard these stories from other people when I was little, from my friends in elementary school when they would talk about church. I never went to church. I was never religious, and neither were my parents. My mother always told me that being spiritual was more peaceful than being religious. She would say religion is tainted; stay true to yourself and when this life is over you will be rewarded. Those words are what helped me stay myself while living in ghetto hell. It was why everyone thought I was stuck up. I was staying true to myself. I refused to be sucked into that mess.

As I walked I found a flat rock placed next to one of the spokes off the river. I sat cross-legged on the rock and watched the water flow. It was very relaxing. As I watched the water, I heard hoofs again. I looked up to see a unicorn. It wasn't

Perilus; this unicorn wasn't what I was expecting. I guess stories made me believe unicorns were always white with white mains; this one was white with grey spots and had a bluish silver main and tail. This one was female; I tired not to startle her as she walked up to me. I just sat and marveled at her beauty. I thought she was going to get a drink, like Perilus had the first time I saw him, but she stopped in front of me and looked me directly in the eyes.

She huffed, it sounded like a content sound. It reminded me of the sound some people make when they sit down after standing too long.

"Are you her?"

I heard someone say. I looked around, but there was nobody there.

"Please don't be frightened."

This time I noticed something odd about what I was hearing. I wasn't hearing it through my ears. It was almost like they were my own thoughts but I wasn't thinking them. I looked back at the unicorn and felt my mind go blank.

I was completely dumbfounded. Was I really hearing the unicorn's thoughts? Holy crap!!!

"Is that . . . . Am I hearing you?" I finally stammered.

"Yes, some are talented with the gift of hearing our thoughts. I thought if you were really her you would be one of them and it seems I was right." she thought.

"Her who?" was all I managed to ask. I was still a little in shock. Even after all I had seen today, I was no where close to being prepared for this.

"Amelinda's daughter." was her response

"Could she hear you too?" I asked. It was nice to meet someone else who knew my mother. Maybe this is why I felt the need to be here. The creatures here knew my mother and maybe I could find out more about her.

"*Yes, all of your people can. You are gifted with a purity which allows communication. Don't you know yourself?*"

"What's your name?" I asked. It may have seemed random but I was getting somewhere, well eventually.

"*Eilzy, why do you ask?*" the unicorn's thoughts seemed confused by my sudden question.

"Well, first, I thought that if we were going to have a conversation than we should have each others names. I am Jenelle. Second, you seem to know more about me than I know about you. I am not aware of much about me considering my mother died ten years ago, which I am sure you know. So if you are going to fill me in then please continue."

"*You don't feel a pull towards the energies of the teeming life around you at all times?*" She asked instead "*Well then maybe the hopes in you are misleading. I am sorry to have bothered you. I must be going now.*" and she turned to leave

"Wait!" I cried "You didn't answer my question."

"*You never asked one, Goodbye Jenelle. I hope to see you soon, as I hope you are as talented as your mother.*" and with that she disappeared.

I sat and thought for a minute. Huh, I guess I never actually asked a question. But the conversation did raise even more questions, not only about this place and what I was doing here but also about me. She said all of my people had this purity. My people? She was talking about my pull towards life around me, was she talking about my love for nature, or something else?

And then there was the nonsense about a hope for me? Was there more of a reason for me to be here then Arhea promising my mother?

I was going to have to be on guard from here on out. I really want to trust everyone here but this just kept getting weirder. So I will stay on guard and collect as much information as possible.

I rose from the rock and started walking towards the tree again. I wasn't sure how long Arhea would be gone, or how long before she sent someone to check on me. I found my way back easy enough. I sat in the chair I sat in earlier for lunch. I watched the streams of sunlight play in the leaves. Judging where the sun was shining in it must be about two. Today had been the longest day of my life. And there was more to come. I wonder if, when I go to sleep tonight, I will wake up and this will all have been a dream after all. That would be disappointing, even with the suspicions I have. I really like it here, I just hope whatever they want from me wont be too much. If it isn't a lot they are asking, maybe I can do it, if it means I can stay here. But if it is more than I can handle will I be able to tell them no? I wasn't so sure the answer was yes, so the only question left is what am I going to do? I felt like I was talking myself in circles, it was kind of making me dizzy. Not in the literal sense, but in the pit of my stomach I had that same feeling.

"Excuse me, would you be Jenelle?" a soft voice called. I looked and saw someone standing there. I was so lost in thought I didn't even see her come in. She looked similar to Arhea. She was shorter by quite a bit, maybe five-four, but she was absolutely beautiful, and had the same strange green tint. Her skin was a little darker; her eyes however were a shocking color of pink. "Hello, I am Acacia, I was sent to check on you. Is there anything you need?" she asked.

"No thank you I am fine for now." I responded. Maybe I could get her to talk to me though "Do you want to keep me company?" I asked trying to find the best way to get more information.

"I can stay for a minute if you would like. I do have a few things to attend to though, so I won't be able to stay for too long." She replied.

"Everyone seems to be busy, is that just today or everyday?"

"Well, I am sure not everyone is busy, but those whose paths you would cross would be busy. You are in the working section of the garden. Most of us show our gratitude to Arhea by assisting in different jobs around the garden. Mostly keeping the plant life happy and healthy and providing what's needed for food and homes. Plus most of us couldn't resist anyway. We couldn't ignore the pull." She smiled at me "Some provide aide in other areas such as working the fields, preparing the food and building or repairing the homes. Then there are some who keep to themselves. I am sure they show their appreciation in other ways." the look on her face made it seem like she was trying to convince herself more than me. But she didn't seem to need much prodding to get information out of her. Maybe this will be easier than I thought.

"Do you do this all the time? I mean do you ever have down time?" I asked trying to get to my questions gradually and as smooth as possible. I also wanted to ask about her comment on resisting the pull, but wasn't sure how to phrase that yet.

"We work when the light is best, as the sun sets we head to our homes. We take two days off out of every seven. Some spend time together, others prefer to be alone. We have celebrations for many reasons where most of us get together to eat and dance. I am sure there will be one sometime over the next few nights to celebrate your arrival."

"What sort of reasons do you celebrate? And why is my arrival reason for celebration?" Maybe this question will get me the answers I need.

"We celebrate a bountiful harvest, we celebrate birth and life, unions, and well basically anything we can find. "She smiled and continued "There are two reasons to celebrate your arrival, first, we celebrate all newcomers and second you're the daughter of Amelinda returned to your rightful home. That is a joyous occasion." she replied. Well that wasn't the information I was hoping for.

"My rightful home?" maybe if I keep asking questions I can get something explained to me.

"Your mother was born here, your people are here. Being here is your birth right. You are not only welcomed but destined to be here." She answered. Again with the "my people" thing. Maybe she will tell me more than Eilzy.

"My people? What do you mean?" I made sure to make it an actual question this time.

"Your mother's parents and siblings. I am sure you will meet them later this evening. Arhea shouldn't be too far off now. So if you will excuse me I have to finish my work before the sun sets." She rose gracefully and left the willow.

I have family here. My mother may be gone forever but her parents and siblings? I might not have gotten the information I particularly wanted from Acacia but she did give me something. Something I hadn't had the chance to think about yet.

It wasn't too much longer after Acacia left that Arhea came into the clearing under the willow. Her small dress seemed dirty and singed in places. Looking at her, made me wonder what happened to her, but also made me a little glad I didn't go with her. She didn't look shaken like I would assume someone with that appearance should look. She smiled at me when she came in.

"Jenelle, I hope your wait wasn't uncomfortable. If you will excuse me for a moment I am going to go clean up a little before we continue the day." She stepped to the other side of the willow and I heard splashing water, leaves rustling, and some sound that was unidentifiable.

When she came back around she was wearing a longer gown made of the same material and looked stunning again.

"Sorry, I warned you of the danger. I guess I got a little to close." She laughed at herself. "If you are ready we need to check on the harvest before I take you to your village."

"I'm ready." and I stood up to follow her out.

We went out the same way as when we went to the meeting. We walked though the clearing for the meeting and down one of the walkways going further in the trees.

CHAPTER 4
HOME

We walked in silence for quite a while. I didn't know what to expect. I assumed we were going to the fields, because that was actually on the agenda for the day and she said she was checking the harvest, but I was prepared for anything.

"After we go to the fields I will finally be able to show you where you are staying." She said breaking the silence. "I am sure this has been a long day for you and you probably would like to rest and come to terms with all you have seen."

I don't know why or where it came from, maybe my brain had had to much to deal with today, whatever the reason I blurted out "What hopes do people have for me? And why do you and everyone else keep staring at me funny?"

She didn't seem concerned by my questions; she smiled "We stare at you because of how much you look like your mother. And the hopes are mixed. Some hope you will take after you mother and fill her lost role." She answered.

I felt a little better. She actually answered my questions, for one thing, but she didn't seem like my questions were rude either. I was worried that I wouldn't be able to get an answer. I also thought the hopes for me would be a lot more. That really wasn't asking much at all. So maybe I can stay here for a while.

I could see a break in the trees up ahead that seemed to lead into a vast clearing. Arhea slowed her pace a minuscule amount but enough for me to notice.

I was completely dumbfounded when we walked into the fields. At least half of the people here were completely human. The rest were a mixture of the other creatures here. Some fairies, elves, the ones who looked like Arhea only shorter, and then there were some I hadn't seen before. They were graceful but didn't seem to hold their figures, they sort of blurred when they moved. I didn't have even the faintest idea of what they were but since I was mostly decided on the fact I was staying I assured myself that I would find out.

One of the humans walked up to us then. She was pretty, but nothing compared to Arhea. She was older, but not old in the sense of wrinkles and gray hair, she gave off the sense of knowledge and maturity. She had a defined bone structure, short blond hair, and blue eyes. It was human pretty.

"How are the fields Faylynn?" Arhea asked the woman.

"They are well Arhea. The harvest is bountiful beyond our hopes." She answered and then she turned to me. "You must be Jenelle. You look just like your mother." She said to me. I was surprised. She was the first person to speak directly to me, in front of Arhea at least.

"Yes, and you are not the first person to tell me that today." I replied with a rueful smile.

"I am glad you are here, when I heard of your birth I wondered if I would ever get to meet my granddaughter, but wasn't hopeful." She said tenderly.

My jaw dropped. So this was my mother's mother. I don't know what I expected, I had been told she was here, I guess I figured there would be more of a formal introduction. I just stood there with half of my smile left on my face. I felt frozen in place; I couldn't change my expression or say anything.

"I'm sorry; I suppose I should have said that a little gentler than I did. Unfortunately I can not go back and change that." She smiled at me then looked to Arhea.

"Well, since we managed to get that covered quickly," Arhea said, and then looked at me "I am going to leave you. Faylynn," Faylynn gave her an odd look," I mean your grandmother, will show you where you will be staying." she waited, looking at me for a response.

"Alright, I suppose I will see you around then Arhea" I stammered, still dumbfounded, barely thinking about what I was saying. "Thank you for everything." I added. I really did appreciate her bringing me here, even if today had been strange it was still amazing.

"Yes, I will see you and you are very welcome." after that she turned to leave.

"Well . . . .?" was all I managed to get out. I wasn't sure what to say. I had a million questions for Faylynn; I just didn't know which to start with.

"First, how are you feeling?" she asked casually.

"I'm O.K." I responded wondering if I didn't look O.K.

"I have information for you that I am not sure whether it has been shared with you, and if it hasn't I don't want it to overwhelm you." She stated bluntly with a very matter of fact tone.

"I started my day a little overwhelmed, so please let me know, just hopefully you wont mind my reaction. I haven't done too well with that today; as you saw before." I warned.

"Have you been told what we are?" she asked.

"No, I guess not, why what are we?" I asked trying to prepare for anything but not sure if my mind was broad enough.

"We are Fae. Do you know what that is?" she seemed like she was trying to slowly fill me in to make up for her bluntness before.

"Nope, I have no idea." I admitted as I braced myself.

"A fae is a human with fairy magic. We are able to communicate with plants and animals and have some healing abilities. There are more details to it but that is the gist of it." She explained.

This probably should have surprised me, but it actually made sense. I have always preferred to be around plants and animals. Plus I was really good at growing plants. I could hear the unicorn and according to her it was a gift. It explained a lot that never really made sense to me.

"Huh." was my brilliant response. "Well then . . . ." I didn't know what else to say.

Faylynn laughed "Alright, we need to finish up here then we can go home." she said. I don't know why but when she said 'home' I felt . . . . right? Like the word actually meant something here, more than just the place I had to live.

"Is there anything I can do to help?" I asked

"Not today, we are mostly done. I just have to check in the orchard over there" She pointed to the groupings of fruit trees "And as long as they are done we can go. Being the leader of the fae, Arhea thought it best to put me in charge of the fields." She smiled and winked at me. "Wait here." she said then walked to the orchards.

So not only was she my grandmother but she was also the leader of the fae. I guess that sort of made me special too, at least to the fae.

She came back fairly quickly. "They are done as well, let us get going." she gestured for me to follow. I did and we started to walk away from the fields. It wasn't just the two of us; almost everyone from the field came with us, the blurry people being the exception. The fairies veered off after a while, the ones who looked like Arhea left here and there, and then it was just the people and the elves. There were a couple of the horse people too. I hadn't seen them in the fields, so I guess they were in the orchards.

"I have a question and I am afraid it might be offensive." I stated as quietly as possible to Faylynn.

"Please ask. I am sure the people here will understand." She replied.

Okay, I hope she is right about that. "What are those people who were kind of blurry?" I asked. I was uncomfortable with my question and it showed in my voice but I really wanted to know.

She laughed. "They are elementals, they associate with the elements and so their shapes shift in and out of human form to element form, that's why they blur." At least she didn't seem offended by my question.

We came to a veil of plants. It made a curtain like the willow did but this was a mixture of leaves and flowers' like it was handmade not grown. Faylynn parted the veil for me to walk through and we were in what looked like a little village.

I silently gasped. It was beautiful. The houses looked like they were made out of the forest, but not in the usual sense. The structures didn't look broken or cut but like natural formations, like they grew out of the ground to form houses. Everyone in the group headed towards different buildings, the horse people stopped at the veil. One of them walked towards us. He was looking at Faylynn.

"We are going to sweep the woods, would you please have someone light our homes for us?" he asked in a gravelly voice. It wasn't unpleasant or unfriendly just deep and rough.

"Of course, we will make sure it gets done." she replied. They turned and left after that.

She turned to me; I guess the questions were in my eyes because she said "The centaurs act sort of like our guard. We rarely have troubles but occasionally some of the creatures from the other side of the island find themselves over here. Brutus forces them back to their side of the island, out of Arhea's boundaries, before they can cause mischief." She explained.

Arhea had made a small comment about the other side of the island, but she only mentioned the one person. She hadn't said much about the other creatures, and kind of avoided my question about them. I assume that the creatures there were similar to the ones here. I was pretty sure there were no 'normal' people or animals on this island.

We started walking towards the houses. It looked like a mixture of old fashioned village and suburban houses. We walked to the very end of the, I guess you would call it a road though it was covered in grass. The houses towards the end were shaped a little different. The looked a little like farm houses made out of the same material.

"I apologize for the delay but we will light the centaur homes, then I will show you your house. After that you are free to do what you wish, without an escort." she turned towards the first house, and opened the door.

As we walked in I couldn't help the short, surprised laugh that came out. The front half of the house looked like a normal set up. There was what I assumed to be a kitchen, dining room, and living room. Towards the back however, there were stable stalls. I assumed this was their bedrooms. She went over towards the kitchen and lit a fire in the big wood stove using a candle that was already lit. This pattern repeated itself for several houses. I stopped counting after seven. When we were finished with the last house, she turned back to me.

"Alright, we are done, now let's get you home." She said. I was a little nervous, and excited. I really hadn't had much time by myself today. I wasn't sure how my mind was going to respond after a day like today when it finally had a chance to think about it in peace.

We walked back towards the smaller houses; she pointed out a few of the houses, naming the people even though I didn't know any of them, and forgot them almost as quickly as she could say them. She also pointed out her own house. Then we walked past the houses altogether. I was a little confused until we came to a small cottage. It was beyond belief. It had a small fence that separated it from the rest of the woods. Inside the fence was a collection of every flower I knew of, and some I had never seen before. There was an apple tree of to the side of the house, and a rose bush climbing the wall on the opposite side of the house. I wasn't even sure what to think. Was this where I was staying?

To confirm the question in my head, Faylynn said "This was your mother's house. Nobody has lived here since she left nor have they changed anything. I thought it fitting that this should be your house."

"My house?" I felt a little fuzzy. I was going to live in the house my mother lived in. "Am I going to be living here alone?" I asked. I was used to being mostly alone, but didn't expect this much. Having my own house to top off being here in the most beautiful place anyone could ever imagine seemed like I was taking too much.

"For the most part, everyone lives alone. The exceptions in this village are couples and families." She explained "If you would prefer not to live here I do have an extra room at my house. I just figured you would like it here." The way she said it seemed like she was afraid I didn't like it.

"Oh no, I love it. I just don't want to take away from someone else." I explained to remove any doubt she had.

"Everyone has a house, don't worry." She looked relieved that I liked it here, as if there could be any other option. "If you need anything, come find me in the village square." then she left me alone.

I walked slowly towards the house. There was a footpath, made up of randomly shaped slate stones that led to the front door. I was moving slowly, trying to take it in. As I opened the door I noticed the hinges looked like tree roots, and they weren't made like a normal door hinge, the root just bent without breaking or looking strained.

Inside was even more unbelievable than outside. The kitchen was small, but perfectly proportioned. There was a bowl of fruit on the counter. It opened up to a little breakfast nook. The cushions on the chairs and bench for the table were made out of some blue material. I walked over and ran my hand across it. It was silk. I had never had anything so luxurious in my entire life. In the center of the table was a small, empty, crystal vase for flowers.

The living area had a small couch and chair made out of the same blue silk. There was a small table placed between them. There was a bookshelf in the corner but the shelves were bare. The walls were also empty.

There were two doors off of the living room. I opened one, and it was a bathroom. The bathroom had a small mirror with a shelf underneath stocked with what looked like bottles and boxes. I went over to see what they were. The boxes had jewelry made of the most beautiful stones. The bottles weren't labeled; I opened one to see what it was. As soon as the lid was off the entire bathroom smelled like roses. I closed the bottle, and the scent lessened but still lingered in the bathroom.

I went to go through the other door. It was the bedroom. There was an armoire in the corner, a full length mirror, a low hook holding a robe, and a canopy bed with a chest at the foot of it. The canopy was made out of the same flower veils that hid the village from the forest. In the armoire there were dresses that looked similar to the one I had seen Arhea wearing. Some were tiny, scanty little things, others looked like formal gowns. There was also a bunch that looked like sun dresses. In the bottom, there were sandal type shoes. I checked the drawers, there were night gowns and under garments. Looking at all of this stuff made me remember I had brought some of my stuff with me when I had left my fathers house. I wonder where it all was. I would have to ask someone tomorrow so I could bring them here. I am still wearing the jeans and t-shirt I left my house in the outside world in. The jeans are dirty and tore up from being in my hiding spot, and I have been walking through the trees here all day today.

I felt wide awake and completely exhausted at the same time. I decided that I probably should get to sleep. I am sure that the surprises aren't over yet. It would take me a while to get used to things here.

I had done quite a bit of walking, so I decided to take a shower first. Showers usually relaxed me, and I was hoping it would help me fall asleep. Going to the bathroom I checked to make sure I wouldn't be thwarted by a lack of running water. To my relief it wasn't a problem. It did help relax me a small amount and I even felt a little like myself again. After today I felt like I didn't know who I was.

When I was done, I felt relaxed enough to possibly get some sleep, I was still on edge but it was lessened. I got dressed in one of the little night gowns in the dresser drawer, it fit perfectly. I lay down on the bed. I was momentarily distracted by how soft the sheets were, and how comfortable the bed was. It was beyond comfortable after sleeping on a lumpy twin mattress. I felt like I was on a cloud. As I was lying there I had a thought that made me giggle. I was home, a home where not only was I wanted but I wanted to be here. It was beautiful and magical and perfect. It was the right place for me to be. I had never thought I would belong anywhere. With that I floated into sleep.

CHAPTER 5
SOCIETY

The plain around me was blurry and there was nothing but emptiness. I started to wander trying to find something, anything. I just kept wondering where the forest was, or the colorless tainted neighborhood around my father's house. I walked around for a minute that seemed to have no end and no beginning. Nothing changed. Then I heard a light thrumming. Almost like a tapping. It was soothing and rhythmic, almost hypnotic. The emptiness around me started to fade.

As I got closer and closer to waking up, I continued to hear the rhythmic thrumming. It sounded like someone drumming their fingers on a table. I finally realized it was a light knocking on the door. I got out of bed and stretched as I called, "Be there in a minute." I felt extremely rested. The fact that I felt so rested was both a new feeling and extremely surprising at the same time. New because no matter how long I slept I never felt rested when I woke up before this place. Surprising because the dream I had wasn't exactly a nightmare but tainted with stress and fear.

I was extremely surprised and pleased that I was still in the house that had belonged to my mother and that all the strange and wonderful things that had happened the day before wasn't a dream.

I grabbed the robe and covered myself before going to answer the door.

It was a woman, with short brown hair, green eyes, and fair skin. She was short and thin. She was pretty and was another one who looked completely human. She didn't look familiar but she looked at me with recognition, almost like she had known me all my life.

"Good morning Janelle." she said, like we were good friends.

I was still groggy because I had just woken up and confused by this overly friendly visitor. I guess that expression showed on my face because she went on.

"You grandmother sent me to come see if you were awake yet. She wants to know if you would like to help in the fields today. Almost everyone is there and if you wanted to join us I can show you the way." She explained very quickly. Well this explains why she was here but doesn't explain the tone or look.

"Yes, I would like to help but I need a few minutes to get ready." I responded "If you would like to wait . . . ." I gestured toward her hoping I could at least get a name.

"Oh!" she exclaimed "How silly of me, I am Alalia." She introduced herself with a small bow that made me a little uncomfortable. It took me a slow minute to register where I had heard that name before. Then it clicked. This was the friend of my mothers that had been watching over me.

"Well its pleasure to finally meet you." I respond whole heartedly. I really was happy to finally meet the woman who has supposedly watched over me my whole life. At the same time I was a little irritated at some of the things she let happen but decided I should probably talk to her and get her side of it before I let any negative emotion towards her take too strong a hold of me. "If you would like to wait feel free to come in, I should be ready in a minute or two." as I said this I moved to the side and gestured for her to come in. She passed me gracefully and went to sit on one of the chairs.

I got dressed quickly in one of the sun dresses, put on a pair of sandals, and headed to the bathroom. I looked at myself in the mirror and was surprised at my reflection. I was so used to the look that I thought was permanent on my face that my expression alone caught me off guard. I had spent most of my life on guard, ready for something bad to happen to me. Here I feel safe and it has made my worry lines soften, my face isn't as tight as it usually was. Also, the look in my eyes was different. I used to be able to see the fear and skepticism in my eyes, now there was something else there. Hope, maybe?

After I resettled myself I rinsed my mouth ran my fingers through my hair and walked back to the front of the house where Alalia waited for me.

She looked up and smiled at me. "Are you ready?" she asked.
"Yes, thank you"

She stood and started to walk to the front door so I followed.

She was very bubbly, and fluid. As she flitted forward I realized how quickly we were moving. The pace I had to keep was quick but not rushed. At this rate we would make it to the fields in no time.

I decided this walk was the best chance I was going to get to talk to her and decide how much I was going to hold her responsible for. I tried to think of a way to ease up to it or at least not sound accusing. We wouldn't have much time so I started in by asking "So did you watch me my whole life?"

"Yes, I went originally to watch over your mother until she was ready to return home. Our kind seems fit more for nature and the outside world destroys so much of their natural resources I didn't think it would take very long. I underestimated her will power." She replied. Although she did seem to have a sad undertone of missing my mother her response still seemed a little selfish.

Since I was irritated it was hard to remember not to be accusing and I blurted out "Well you didn't do very well at taking care of either of us." I didn't yell necessarily but my tone was harsh. She flinched and I almost immediately felt bad about saying it.

She replied in a sad, broken, small voice "I know, I told them I wouldn't do a very good job." she looked like she might start crying.

I tried to use a more gentle voice when I asked "What exactly were your instructions?"

She straightened up and got a hard look in her eyes, almost defensive "I was to follow her to the outside world, stay with her as often as possible, not interfere with her plans or decisions unless it was life threatening or threatened exposure of us or our location, and make sure no matter what that she was happy. The last two are what conflicted. Her staying was becoming life threatening. The outside worlds lack of nature and her needs and elements conflicting with what she wanted was starting to make her ill, but her happiness carrying you and having your dad take care of you both, planning their life together, making her refuse to return home. She thought she was strong enough to handle it, get over her illness. Your genetics hold a series of benefits and most of you have the ability to heal and she thought that with you she would be able to overcome it. Your abilities were still extremely underdeveloped and she lacked the resources she needed. When she passed you were still unaware of your abilities or much about your self for that matter. Your dad suffered from a broken heart that killed him, in the sense that the man who your mother loved no longer existed. I stayed to keep you alive and out of harm's way until you were old enough to be brought here." She bowed her head. The sorrow of the story took away her bubbliness. The story also gave some new information about myself.

"So you never left me or my mother?" I asked feeling bad for bringing her up and selfish for wanting her to tell me more. I had to know though.

"I did, once to announce that your mother was pregnant with you and getting married, again when you were born, then when she got sick to try to figure how to help here since my instructions conflicted. A few times I returned here trying to get Arhea to agree to bring you early and then finally when you walked out of your dad's house and hid to tell her that it was time." She explained.

This explanation gave me a lot to think about but our walk was half over and I wanted to know more before it was too late. I could sort through it all later.

"What happened with your trips back?" I asked. She didn't need much prodding one question brought on a slew of information.

"The first time there was spectacle of the pregnancy before marriage and discussions of informing your dad about everything. The verdict was no information. Both your mother and you were allowed to know and return here but not him. Although she saw something in him, he was not pure enough to be allowed and they feared he could be corrupted. This proved true. You were not to be told until you were eighteen per your mothers instructions' and we were not to force her home since it was against her will."

"What about me and my life in the outside world?" I could hear my tone was getting snippy again but this was the crucial question on whether or not I was going to hold her responsible for anything that happened to me.

"I was not allowed to approach you, I could only assist if things were critical and even then I had to take circuitous routes to protect you, because I was under the rules given by your mother. If you were in danger of the beings around your home I could alter or end the path they were on. I could use their resources such as your police or even other evil beings to change the course of actions. I was allowed to deal with people who dealt with you as well, like your employer, to help protect you and I had an informer who knew what was going to happen who helped me but they were around less often so I sometimes had to work quickly with no advance warning or outside help." she explained.

I decided that her orders and lack of help made it so my life was not her fault. She tried and I know how hard trying to take care of myself and father was, I couldn't imagine being in a strange world with little to no help while trying to keep someone else safe. The entire time I have been here there has always been someone there to help me. These thoughts made me soften up. I wanted to help more since I have been so selfish, untrusting, and sometimes even a little mean since I got here.

I decided to change the subject completely for the time being "What I am going to be doing in the fields?" I asked

"Whatever you like I suppose, you could tend the gardens, work in the orchards, or collect water. If you wanted you could just sit and watch or you can talk to the workers, help give them what they need." She answered. As we walked she slowly turned back to herself, it was like the weight and sorrow of our conversation was seeping out of her. By the time we reached the fields it was like it never happened, except the bits of information I gathered. The first part of my plan is to be helpful and less hostile the second is to gather as many pieces of information possible and piece them all together.

I mostly just walked around and watched what others were doing. Sometimes I would talk to the workers but mostly just polite conversations. The day went by quickly and aside from my conversation with Alalia this morning I didn't gather any new information. My grandmother checked in on me from time to time but the harvest season was almost over so she was very busy. On our walk back from the fields was the first time I was really able to talk to her.

"Do you know what happened to the stuff I had with me the night I came here?" I asked her

"No but I am sure Alalia would know, let's stop and ask her." She suggested.

"Ok, and is there any way I could get a journal or even paper. I want to start writing my experiences down, you know, try to sort it all out." I tried to be honest without giving away too much of my intentions.

"We will find your stuff, and I will get you a journal." She smiled at me and it seemed my explanation on why I needed a journal was enough.

We walked into the village and up to one of the houses. My grandmother knocked and in what seemed like no time at all Alalia answered the door. She looked surprised to see us standing there. "What can I do for you?"

"Apparently Jenelle brought stuff with her when she left her home in the outside world and she wanted to know where it was." my grandmother answered.

"Oh, yes I will go retrieve them and deliver them to your home." Alalia said.

"Perfect" my grandmother replied to her then she turned to me "And I will go get you what you asked for." She turned and walked away.

Since I was left alone I decided to walk around the village and see how things worked here. I hadn't noticed on my first walk through but some of the buildings were stores. I went inside one and an elemental was standing behind the counter. I was nervous and excited to actually talk to one.

"What do you use for money here?" I asked

She laughed a breathy sigh and answered "We do not use money; our services are given on a sort of credit. We give what we have or our knowledge in exchange for a promise that the debt will be repaid when needed. If I give my services I do not tally who owes me, but all the same it will be repaid." She answered. Her voice was quiet and wispy, like the wind. I assumed her element was air.

"What services do you offer?" I asked to try to understand each place in case I need it.

"Information, the winds tell me things most cannot hear. If someone plans to travel to the outside world I can tell them what is going on to an extent. Weather, mostly. The winds are excellent at telling when there will be rains, floods, droughts, and other natural causes. But they also prove to know their fair share of secrets that can be passed on to those in need of the information."

"Oh" again with my brilliant responses.

I left that store and entered another a little ways down. This one had plants and liquids packaged on shelves covering all of the walls. The woman looked human so I assumed she was a fae, although she wasn't very attractive. I asked "What are all the bottles and packages for?"

"What else is a witch good for if it isn't to make remedies?" She relied.

A witch? This is something I hadn't expected, even in a world of mythical characters. I tried to hide my surprise and asked "Remedies for what?"

She smiled "Mostly for healing, most of the creatures don't need normal remedies but if someone gets hurt some of these will heal wounds or rid a body of infections. Sometimes a fae will want to venture to the outside world and get contaminated so when they return home I give them one. I do have others for a wide range of other needs but they are very rarely used." She answered.

"So one of your remedies could have healed my mom?" I asked

"Yes, my remedies never fail." She answered confidently.

"Then why didn't you send one to her in the outside world?"
I asked. I was angry with this woman; she could have saved my
mom.

"She didn't want anything from me. Your mother and I
had . . . . a few disagreeing points that couldn't be reconciled.
Arhea asked me for one and I didn't refuse but Amelinda
said she would manage. I guess she was wrong, again." she
answered.

I was furious with how she spoke about my mother. I had
never met anyone who had any negative feelings for her. This
was not normal; I turned and walked out without another word.
I couldn't handle it. I just started walking I had no idea what
direction I was heading. I stopped after about fifteen minutes of
blind walking. I was still in the village I think. Everything looked
almost the same except the houses were much smaller. As I
walked it got even smaller until it was like I was in a miniature
village. The small people with butterfly wings were flitting
about. One of them flew up to me until she was at my eye
level. She looked small compared to those still flying around or
walking. With her being so close I could tell she was a child, she
looked almost like a toddler.

"Hello, what are you doing in the fairy village?" she asked in
a tinkling voice. I should have known they were fairies. I guess
while I am here I need to remember what I can about mythical
creatures and learn what I don't know.

"I was just walking around. Am I not allowed to be here?" I
asked.

"Oh no you are allowed to go where you want but most
everyone else doesn't bother coming to this part of town.

Considering you are all too big to fit in the houses." she answered with a giggle.

"Oh, well I would like to look around. Will you be my guide?" I asked

She giggled and answered "Yes, what would you like to see?" she asked. She seemed excited that I wanted her to show me around but I had no idea what she could show me. For the reasons that she pointed out I can't really look in the houses. Then I had an idea.

"Do you have any shops around this part?" I asked clinging to one of the only things I could think of.

"Yes, we have two. One is for clothing and the other is for treats." She answered. Well the clothing one wouldn't do me any good but the treats one might.

"Will you show me the treats shop?" I asked. She started flying forward so I followed. I noticed some of the houses were in the trees, placed along the trunks and on the branches. She flew to one of the buildings hanging from a branch. I was relieved to see that there was no front to the building so I would actually be able to see. When I walked up the fairy in the building gawked at me. I guess she wasn't expecting anyone, especially not someone of my size.

"How can I help you?" she asked.

"I was wondering what kind of treats you had?"

"We have honey suckle drops, honey comb, and sweet berries today." she answered.

"May I please have a piece of honey comb?" she gave me a piece and I smiled.

"Well I should get back home, thank you both." I said to them and left.

I walked back in the direction where the houses were smaller but not tiny trying to find my way back home. I took notice in all the creatures I passed until I found my way back home. Some were harder to put a name to than others and some seemed to be a combination of others I saw.

When I walked into my house I noticed my bag and a journal on the table. They must have dropped it off when I was in the fairy village.

CHAPTER 6
JOURNAL

First I went through my bag and put my stuff up. My clothes went with the other clothes in the bedroom armoire. It was nice to have a little more variety and normality. My bathroom stuff went into the bathroom. I took the time to actually brush my hair and teeth. I put my jewelry box in the bathroom with the other boxes. I couldn't think of a reason for anything in my purse so I decided to put it in the chest at the foot of my bed. When I went to open it I was surprised to see it wasn't empty. It held a small wooden box, several bouquets of dead flowers, and a journal. I took out the box and journal placed my purse under the flowers and walked to the living room.

Before I sat on the floor I grabbed my journal. I sat on the living room floor, placed the two journals in front of me and opened the box. There was a pen, pictures and several pieces of paper. I took the pen out and tested it on the inside of my journal, it still worked. This is good because I don't have a pen. I am sure there was another around here or I could at least get one if I needed but this is just easier. Then I looked at the pictures, they were an odd collection of different formats. Some seemed like typical prints from a camera, others looked like paintings. They were of my mother, some of her working in the fields, some in this house, and then some with other creatures and people from the garden. There was a man in several of them. He was very attractive with dark red hair and grey eyes. He looked familiar but I couldn't place it. I decided to keep these and sorted through the ones I especially liked of her in the house or fields. The ones of her by herself I would find a way to have them framed and hang them up her so I can feel like she is here with me. I pulled out the letters and opened them. I didn't feel like I was intruding, these belonged to my mother and since not only is she no longer here but since this house was left to me. The first letter read:

My dearest Amelinda,

My love for you could never be replaced or replicated. I would follow you to the ends of the earth. I will never understand why you insist on keeping our love from the garden. No hardship you could predict could be worth the turmoil you put on us. Our love is pure no matter how you look at it, no one would contest that, and if they do so be it. Please consider my offer.

Love Indefinitely,
Kynis

So my mother had a secret boyfriend. I wonder how that played out. I hope the letters and her journal explain it. The next letter read:

My dearest Amelinda,

Why must you be so stubborn? There are no secrets of mine you do not hold and I can tell there are things you keep from me. I wish to know everything about you. There is nothing you could tell me that could diminish my love for you. Please understand that I will be by your side for all eternity. Trust me!

Love Indefinitely,
Kynis

So far it doesn't seem like this is playing out very well.

Letter three:

My dearest Amelinda,

How could you let us be so close in body but so distant in heart and mind. I have given you all of my heart, body, mind and soul. Please, let us be honest with each other and honest with those in the garden. I cannot live in secrecy forever but I am determined to be at your side forever. Please understand there is nothing to fear

Love Indefinitely,
Kynis

The last letter read:

My dearest Amelinda,

Please do not do this. Do not leave without me. Allow me to venture to the outside world with you where I can protect you. We can announce our love at last and then share this experience together. Even if you do not wish to announce it we can think of something, let me come with you. Please come speak with me before you do anything.

Love Indefinitely,
Kynis

These letters were confusing and inconclusive. I decided to read my mothers diary next to see if I could get any more information. This might be more than I could gather in bits and pieces from my miscellaneous conversations. Plus from what little I could gather from the letters nobody knew about this secret relationship. I opened my mother's journal and realized almost immediately that it started a little farther back than the letters. This was good. It might help me piece together what was going on better. The first page started with Kynis which was even better. It was what I wanted to know about.

Page one:

Today I spent time with Kynis in the fields. He seems very kind. Most of the wizards I have met seem a little sinister. He seems to have a feel for nature though. I wonder why that is.

Page two:

Kynis came to join me in the fields again. While we worked he told me much about himself. More information than I would have thought anyone would give after such a short time. His feel for nature makes more sense. Apparently his mother was fae. She passed giving birth to him since a pure fae cannot withstand child birth from a pure wizard. His father was skeptical of almost everything but never seemed to have negative comments about his mother.

Three:

I feel Kynis may be growing rather fond of me. Tonight at our harvest celebration he seemed to turn up everywhere. He sat with me at the feast, appeared when I was talking to my mother, even asked me to dance. I accepted out of courtesy but I wonder if that was very wise of me.

Four:

Maybe I am more like my family line than I thought. Although I have never understood the fascination of pairing outside of our species, I do find that I am oddly pleased whenever Kynis does something to gain my attention. When I am around him I feel warm and safe.

Five:

I went for a walk with Kynis tonight. In the woods where no one could see us his actions were less cordial. He guided me along with his hand on the small of my back, brushed my hair back behind my ear, he even complimented me. He told me my eyes could outshine any emerald and my smile could make the moonlight look dull in comparison. I must admit it was very flattering.

Six:

This morning when I woke up there was a bouquet of flowers on my window sill. In them was a note from Kynis. He asked me to meet him by the cavern lake tonight at midnight. This is very much different then the walks we have taken over the last few weeks. I think I am going to go.

Seven:

Last night Kynis professed his love for me. I didn't know what to say. I was so shocked and speechless that I just turned and walked back home. I didn't even look behind myself. I worry I may have hurt him. I am very taken with him but do I really want to start a relationship? Especially one with so much controversy. My mother got sideways glances and whispers flew up until the day my father passed. Even now some people will not deal with her because of her relationship. Fortunately I have not been subjected but do I want to force myself into that scenario. Outside my door was another bouquet with a note that said "meet me". I want to go but I must be better prepared this time.

Eight:

My meeting with Kynis went a little better last night. I confessed I do care for him but thought it would be wiser for us to court secretly and cordially. I do not want to make a mistake that will forever haunt me. He seemed thrilled by the fact that I too have feelings for him, so much so that my request did not bother him. I do hope I will not regret this.

Nine:

Tonight I have been secretly seeing Kynis for three weeks. He has been understanding so far about the secrecy but the cordialness has dropped on his part. When we walk he puts his arm around my waist or tries to hold my hand. Flowers are left on my window sill almost every day. And tonight before we parted he leaned in and kissed my cheek. His kiss was innocent but sent a shiver through me. Not one of fear or cold, it was a new sensation. Maybe I will have no choice but to follow in my family line.

Ten:

The kisses from Kynis have become less innocent and sweet and more passionate. He has moved from my cheek and kisses my lips. Tonight it felt like he kissed me forever but still not long enough. When he stopped I still wanted more.

Eleven:

I finally admitted to myself and to Kynis that I do love him deeply. There is no more denying it when I do not attempt to discourage his physical affection anymore. I even initiate some of the more subtle actions. Kynis was ecstatic but I still want to keep our love a secret for now. I will be sixteen soon and at that age I will be considered able to live on my own or marry if I choose. I will rethink the situation when the time comes.

Twelve:

I have moved into my house now. Kynis visits me at night when no one could walk by and see. He no longer understands my desire for secrecy. I tried to explain what it could do to us in the garden but he seems unperturbed.

Thirteen:

Kynis stayed the night with me last night. It was a strange and wonderful feeling having him so close to me all night. My body was full of a warm pulling sensation that seemed to draw myself to him. He pushed for us to tell the garden about us again but I declined. This morning after he left I found a letter from him.

Fourteen:

Kynis doesn't know my plans to venture to the outside world within the year. I am afraid to tell him because this is a journey I plan to take alone. I want to experience a new life to see if there is more freedom there. I know he can tell I am hiding something from him because today there was another letter when he left.

Fifteen:

Kynis has stayed almost every night since the first night. We sleep in the same bed and it feels like we are growing into a more serious relationship. I am not sure if this is what I want right now. I think tonight I will not have him stay.

Sixteen:

My plan to not let Kynis stay failed horribly. We lay in my bed holding each other like any other night when he leaned in and kissed me passionately on the mouth. When he pulled away he whispered in my ear that he loved me. He then kissed me along the side of my neck. With out giving myself conscious permission to do so I gave all my physical love to him.

Seventeen:

Although I know I shouldn't until we are married I cannot help giving Kynis myself. It is wonderful and fulfilling but is not enough for him. He left me another letter today.

And the last page read:

How could I have been so naïve to think my physical love for Kynis would go without repercussions I must make my journey to the outside world now before it is too late. I have already presented my case before Arhea and she has agreed to let me go. I must take company so I chose Alalia because even if she finds out she will not tell anyone if I ask her not to. Kynis left me a letter but I cannot agree to his requests. If I wait any more than a few weeks it will be too late and everyone will know. I will find a partner in the outside world and we will have a family. I may or may not return in the future. I will not put a child through witnessing what I did growing up. The judgment is too much here. Too many people already have suspicions about Kynis and me. It must end. I will leave a note for Kynis telling him and only him the truth. I will tell him I love him and whatever I might feel for anyone else will never compare to my love for him.

!!!!!!!!!!! . . . . The silent alarms in my head would let up. Could she mean, did this just say, my mother was pregnant before she left here. I am an only child if this is true then my father is not my father! My father is here in the garden and his name is Kynis. I must find a way to meet him and I need to know more. I will build a relationship with someone who I can confide in and will pull for as much information as I possibly can.

For now I just made a list of information in my journal. First was the list of things I have gathered: I could tend to plants, hear animal's thoughts, and there are thoughts I can heal and have other abilities. Then there is the information from my mother's journal. I might have a different father than the one I thought. I am not only fae but am unsure how far back the pairings with other species goes. And there is judgment on my family because of their choices. I need to find out what other abilities I may or may not have, if Kynis is my father, and what other species I might have in my blood. Getting this sorted out is going to be tricky and may take a while. I felt over whelmed and exhausted. I crawled into bed fully dressed and fell into an uneasy sleep. I had dreams of the turmoil on my mother, judgment on my family, and then my body transforming into parts of the creatures I have seen in the garden. I startled awake often and every time I fell back to sleep it was the same thing.

CHAPTER 7

INFORMATION

The sun was finally rising after I woke up from a dream where my body was part horse and I had wings. I decided to lie in bed and try to collect myself. The onslaught of information over the past two days was starting to wear down my mind. It had been the longest two days of my life but still the best since my mother had died.

The sun was fully in the sky before I decided to get up. I took a shower which made me feel a little more like myself. I brushed my hair and teeth, and then headed to the kitchen. I grabbed an apple and sat at the table trying to organize my plan. I need to figure out who I should talk to, who would be able to give me answers, and how to prove what was true or not. I also needed to figure out how to ask my questions. While I was sitting there I could hear some kind of commotion in the distance. I got dressed in a sundress and sandals and headed out.

As I got closer to the town square I could see everyone was there. Nobody was in the fields and, if anyone, few were even in their houses. I caught sight of Alalia and decided to ask her what was going on.

"Hey Alalia, what's going on?" I half hollered at her as I walked towards her.

"Hello, Jen how are you today? Are you ready for tonight?" she asked

"What is going on tonight that I need to be ready for?" I asked. Her excitement made me feel a little nervous.

"Well we get to have a double celebration tonight. One for your arrival and two because this seasons harvest is over." She replied. "We are in the middle of decorating the square, the centaurs and satyrs are bringing in the tables. The elves and fairies are helping some of the fae and witches prepare the feast, and almost everyone else is here. The rest will join as the day progresses." She explained fully.

I took a mental note of all the creatures she said. This will help me a little bit when I try to get some of my answers. Maybe I could become closer to Alalia. She was already my mother's friend, and I do really like her.

"Is there anything I can do to help?" I asked.

"No you are one of the reasons we are celebrating. You need to start getting ready. You need to be ravishing considering this is half your party." she answered.

"Um . . . Alalia . . . . I don't know how to be ravishing?" I answered a little unsteady. What I was wearing now was one of the prettiest things I have ever dressed in. Usually it was pants and t-shirts for me. Alalia looked at me like she understood the sound in my voice and called for help.

"Cymbeline, get some of the girls for a makeover." she said to one of the girls who's skin was tinted green. Then she turned to me and said "Head home trust me—the girls will beat you there." She smiled and turned back to her work.

I headed home like I was instructed but as Alalia had predicted there were three of the girls there in front of my house waiting for me. As I approached, Acacia was the first to greet me. "Hello again, these are Cymbeline and Fialka, we are part of the team in charge of appearance here in the garden. We make the clothes and cosmetic products . . . and in this case, help those in need to get ready for big occasions." She explained. "Emerenta and Glykera are preparing your dress. You will meet them shortly." Then she stood there and waited. It took me a minute to get over my fear of the word makeover to realize they were waiting for me to go inside.

"Oh, sorry it's nice to meet you." I said trying to stay polite even though I was still nervous. "So, let's go inside." I suggested. I led the way into the house and they followed. As soon as we were in the house the girls started flitting about. The one I am assuming to be Fialka pulled out a chair next to the table. As I sat down I realized she looked almost exactly like Acacia except instead of pink eyes, hers were violet.

I was listening to them talk as they gathered around me. Acacia seemed to be the one in charge. She was commenting on what needed to be done.

"There isn't much to do," she was saying "she is pretty enough we don't have to use much make up, not like when we do some of the witches" she said to the other girls and they all giggled. "Cymbeline, you start on her hair, but I want it left down. Fialka, you help me with the face." she said and then they were off. Cymbeline was weaving the hair on top of my head and occasionally adding small flowers, and Acacia and Fialka were both working simultaneously on my face. I listened as they talked. I found out that Acacia and Fialka were in fact twins, the three of them were nymphs and the two I hadn't met yet were fae. When they weren't making clothes or helping people get ready they each had a knack for something. The twins were flower experts. They could convince the flowers to give them color, or the glisten out of the morning dew. This alone had my brain flying with questions. Then Cymbeline loved music, she actually had a choir on and off with the mermaids. Again my brain spiraled. I wondered to myself if I would ever get used to this. Two days was hardly enough time to get used to ideas that my brain couldn't even conjure in dreams. Even with that though my spiraling thought were not questioning the possibilities they were explaining, they were trying to figure out if I could learn to do these things, or see them at the very least. The girls kept babbling and working and I tried to retain as much information as possible.

There was a knock at the door, Cymbeline was done with my hair and asked, "Would you mind if I answer the door? You are not quite finished and it is probably Emerenta and Glykera with your dress." she said.

"No that's fine." I replied.

The two other girls came in carrying a silver gown. It was the most beautiful thing I had ever seen. It was slender and shimmering. Emerenta started to explain what it was made out of. "It's woven from the mist of the river and stardust that fell from the skies and was caught by skillful hands. The mermaids helped us collect these materials, and then we had a wizard put a spell on the mist to make it tangible." She explained.

"Which wizard?" Acacia asked "They usually don't like to help us."

"Kynis, of course." Glykera answered.

This stopped any other thoughts in my head. Of course Kynis would help since he was half fae. I had been trying to catch as much information through this as I could about this world but I wasn't prepared for this. I was so stunned to hear his name and then suddenly realized that I still didn't know enough about him. This proved to be a perfect chance to ask some questions without being obvious. "Why don't the wizards usually like to help?" I asked and then added to not let them know I knew anything "And why is that one different?"

"The wizards like to keep to themselves for the most part but Kynis is half fae."

Acacia answered. "He is actually Glykera's half brother. Their mother died giving birth to him." she added. "He helps us with most things but I think that partially because most people won't deal with him. A lot of the people here are not fond of cross breeding. They think each should stick to their own race. I however think that love is stronger than race and it shouldn't matter. There are a few others who agree but the general population here is against it." She explained. This means that if Kynis is my father, then Acacia was my aunt. It was an interesting thought but I would have to think it over later when I was by myself and had a few more facts, like whether or not the journal said what I think it said. So I asked my next question.

"How many people here are mixed?" maybe I could start linking relationships together and figure out what all I am mixed with.

"There are not many, since most are against it there are family lines that mix with other willing species, I heard of one relationship that happened hundreds of years ago that somehow a fae managed to get a wizard to impregnate her with dragon, but according to legend the baby was more dragon and the mother didn't survive." She seemed hesitant to discuss this. I am not sure why but I think part of it was I don't think she wanted out my family to me. I tried again.

"What kind of surviving mixes are there?" I asked maybe I could take a longer route.

"Mostly it is a mix with fae." answered Emerenta. She didn't seem as averse to giving me information "Most of our kind does not see a problem with cross breeding they say it's because how human we are. There is the dragon rumor but it is known that fae have had children with wizards, elementals, merpeople, and nymphs." Ok so these are my main possibilities. But then she added "the problem with it is when we have had children with wizards they can intertwine magic and there have been some found with powers from unicorns, phoenix', sphinx', and even dragons, which is why I think the rumors started." So this added even more information, since, if I am right, I was a cross with not only a cross breed but two, one of them being half wizard raised by a wizard. But my mother never told Kynis so he probably didn't intertwine the magic directly on me. I don't think?

"How do you cross with a mermaid? I mean with the fin and all how does that even work?" I asked. I was intrigued by this conversation and really wanted to keep it going.

"Merpeople are half and half beings already, they have qualities to protect them given by both their human and fish sides. If a merperson in the water they maintain the true form, but under some circumstances, if they are completely dried off they take full human form as a form of self preservation. However, similar to other species, if they are left out of their natural environments for too long they get sick." Emerenta explained.

"Do cross breeds get all the powers of whatever they are mixed with?" I asked trying to keep the conversation casual.

"Not necessarily, a child produced can have both sides' powers; sometimes they get more of one or the other or an even mix of the combination. In some cases, if the cross breeding goes on for more than one generation, the last generation can have a combination of all of the previous mixes simultaneously. Rumor has it that if this was to happen, then that child could also form a strange mixture of the powers forming completely new powers that neither parent had." then she winked at me.

Since Emerenta was the one who explained everything to me in detail I thought she might eventually be a good choice for a friend, a confidant at the very least. Then there was the wink, did this mean she thought that I would be like the rumors? Is this why some people look at me with that strange look? No that couldn't be it, since if Kynis was my father then nobody knew, not even Kynis.

Acacia must have felt this conversation was getting too detailed because she gave a breathy laugh and said "Okay now, back to getting ready."

The girls had me stand up to slide the dress on. It felt like I was standing in nothing but my underwear in flowing water. It was beautiful, elegant, and a little revealing. It was a halter, with a neckline that reached my belly button. The two sides flowed like curtains over each side of my chest until they met. The back was even lower. It was bare up until the point where my back ended. I felt if the dress adjusted at all I would start exposing myself.

The shoes were another complication. They were silver and thin. The heel was almost invisible and at least six inches long. The straps that held them on looked like vines from a tree dyed silver. The girls helped me put them on, criss-crossing the vines from my ankles to my knees.

The last thing was a small bottle Acacia pulled out. "Sit down look up and keep your eyes open. This wont hurt at all but will add the last touch you need." She said. I did as she told me to and she let one cold drop of whatever it was into each of my eyes. I assumed they were some sort of eye drop but wasn't sure exactly what it was for until she said: A drop of dew to make your eyes glisten like the rest of you." then she turned me towards a mirror.

I was startled at my reflection. My hair was in waves with flowers running through it and it hung over my shoulder perfectly. The dress was even more beautiful on then it was in someone's arms. I almost didn't recognize myself. I had a slight shimmer to my body and a twinkle in my eyes thanks to the dew drops.

"Okay, what now?" I asked.

"Well, first, why don't you try to walk around the room? I want to make sure we got the fitting right. If we need to make any adjustments now will be the time to do it." Glykera suggested.

I did as I was asked and walked a few circles around the room; Glykera even had me spin in a few circles to make sure the fabric wouldn't move from side to side on my chest. I felt almost like I was exercising. She made me lift my arms above my head, then point them straight out and swing them from one side to the other. I had to sit down, stand up, bend over, and continue through an entire list of any possible movement I might have to make tonight.

"Fantastic," Acacia cut in "now the last thing is dancing and we should be all set as far as wardrobe checks go."

"Dancing?" I asked alarmed. "I don't dance, so that shouldn't be a problem." I tried to explain.

"If someone asked you to dance would you turn them down?" Acacia asked in reproach.

"Probably, considering I don't know how to dance, I have a valid reason for turning anyone down. The last time I danced it was just a bunch of silly twirling when I was a little girl."

"It is rude, if someone asked you to dance you should always except unless you are already spoken for. That is the only valid reason for turning someone down, and even then a harmless dance can be promised for a later time." Acacia said. She sounded almost offended.

"And what about not knowing how? What do you expect me to do?" I asked getting defensive. "I would make of fool out of both myself and whoever unwillingly subjected themselves to the embarrassment."

I guess Cymbeline didn't like the tension because when she spoke it was with a calming voice saying "We could show you basic steps real quick that could get you through the night so if the situation presents itself you will be able."

"Perfect!" Acacia answered for me. Apparently I wasn't going to have any say in this.

The girls each took turns with me. They were showing me basic moves form each of their own experiences. Fortunately they were all very simple. I had a feeling that if people didn't like my family line of cross breeders then I wouldn't have to worry too much, but since obviously there were some people in the garden that didn't mind I did feel better now that I wasn't going to be completely lost on the dance floor.

"Alright, I think we are done." Acacia said and then gave a successful smile to the other girls.

"Um . . . just to make sure, since apparently I have more to learn about this world than I thought, is there anything else I should know before the celebration starts?" I asked.

"Well the most important thing is not to be rude. If someone offers you a drink or asks to dance, accept. Don't drink too much or eat too much either. Drinking too much juice and eating too much might make you sick, and drinking too much wine might make you do or say things you will regret. Which I am sure you are aware of at least that much since you do have wine in the outside world." Acacia explained.

"Okay anything else?"

"Have fun, it is a celebration and as long as you keep these tips in the back of your mind there is no need to worry. You don't want to ruin your night because you are worried." Emerenta said and smiled at me. I already really liked her.

"The party will be starting as soon as everyone arrives at the square and I think most everyone is already there so let's go get ready really quick girls." Acacia had said to the others and then turned to me "You can head over there when ever you are ready, we will meet you there." Then all of them turned to leave.

After they left I was able to concentrate, which wasn't really a good thing. Besides the over load of information over the last few hours I was scared stiff of making a fool of myself at this celebration. It took me several attempts to breath right before I decided it was best to get it over with.

One final deep breath and a run through of all the tips I was given, especially the dancing tips, and I headed out the door to the town square.

CHAPTER 8

CELEBRATION

I was the last to arrive. I guess my panic attack lasted longer than I thought. Even the girls beat me there, but that wasn't surprising considering they beat me to my house earlier. I wonder how they get around so quickly. The square the looked even more beautiful then this morning and that was a surprise. There were tables surrounding the square leaving the center open for a dance floor. Directly across from me there was a table set a little higher then the rest, like at the meeting. Everything seemed to sparkle. The tables had green silk tablecloths and each had a beautiful centerpiece that looked like a waterfall flowing into a stone bowl with flowers floating in them. In strings above our heads it looked like they had strung stars together to give us lights, and considering the things I heard this morning this was very possibly the case. Arhea was at the high table as well as Faylynn and a couple of others. When she caught sight of me she smiled and waved me over. I walked towards the head table and everyone stared at me.

"You look gorgeous!" Faylynn exclaimed when I reached the table.

"Thank you, Acacia will be happy to hear that." I replied.

The night started with Arhea making a small speech. "Thank you everyone. First of all we had a wonderful harvest season. Everyone enjoy the break over the next few weeks before we start the next cycle." A few people laughed. "Second, I know everyone knows by now that Amelinda's daughter arrived a few days ago. Please try to make her feel welcome all of you. She is unaware of many things in the garden so help her if needed. Enjoy the celebration for this is a double and I have a surprise for all of you later." She sat back down and then two centaurs brought out a very large table already filled with food. They sat it in front of the main table and then turned to leave without a glance in our direction.

Some people came to get food, some paired off and started talking or dancing, and everyone seemed to be looking at me as often as possible.

"Jenelle, have you decided how long you would like to stay here?" Arhea had asked. I had forgotten the last time I had talked to her I had said I could stay for a couple of days.

"I'm still not sure." I answered honestly. "I think everything here is wonderful but am worried that I won't fit in very well here. I was raised in the outside world and things that are done here are very different. I don't want to become a burden to anyone."

"You will not be a burden, and if you would like to stay there are several people here who would be willing to help show you the way. I believe once you get used to it you will find it to be more alike with the outside world then you think. You were raised for half of your life by your mother and she was raised here. From my understanding you were more like your mother than anyone else in the outside world." she answered. It didn't feel like she was trying to persuade me to stay exactly but that she wanted me to want to stay and she was willing to help if I wanted her to.

"You do the education here in the garden right?" I asked. It may have sounded out of context but again, I had a point.

"I do" She answered unsure of what I was looking for.

"Is the education you give here the same as what I received in the outside world?"

"It is similar. I do teach basic math and reading but our language options are different for those who choose to learn them, our history is very different and I teach different people based on their abilities."

"Could you teach me the history and anything else I need to learn that I didn't pick up in the outside world?"

"I would be willing to do this if you choose. I am not the only educator though, some subjects are taught by other creatures since I am not an expert at their abilities. I am sure I could find you a full set of educators at this point though."

I guess if I am going to be here I should do it right. "Ok, will you please do this then?"

"Yes meet me at the willow tomorrow morning when the sun is fully up."

Then I was overtaken by different people greeting me. There were so many I didn't catch their names. I guess I would learn them all eventually. I even danced with a couple of people. Dancing with the nymphs and fae was fairly easy but when Darion asked me to dance it was a little awkward, first because he was still young so he was shorter than me and second because his legs moved different then mine. The food was good, but the wine was strong. I had two glasses before it hit me then my brain was a little fuzzy and I was giggly, which was completely out of character for me. Like most things here the wine must be different than what I am accustomed to in the outside world. I switched to water after that and ate some more to try and soak up the alcohol.

As my brain started to clear up I started watching everyone enjoy the party. Two things caught my eye. First was a young man sitting by the trees on the edge of the square. He was by himself and barely drinking his wine. The thing about him that caught my eye was he was staring at me. Not the glances everyone else gave me, he didn't even have the same mixture of expressions in his eyes. It was a strange stare that made me think he was trying to tell me something. He was extremely attractive and something about the way he looked at me made me want to blush and duck under the table. It was a very odd thing. He was one of the ones who had pointed ears but was tall and slim; he looked sophisticated and graceful even as he stared.

The second thing that caught my eye was Kynis. He was over with Acacia and Fialka talking calmly but he kept looking in my direction and every time I caught the expression in his eyes it was shock. I wonder if he realizes I look like him. I think Kynis is the only thing that could distract me from the man by himself and oddly enough even that wasn't enough to block out the stranger completely.

I tried to form a plan. I wanted to figure out a way to talk with both of them. I could go compliment Acacia on my appearance and be right there with Kynis, I could introduce myself and that should be enough to start a conversation. The other person however would be more difficult. I decided to ask my grandmother who had just returned to the table after dancing.

"Who is that over there by himself?" I asked her. She followed my look and when she realized who I was talking about eyed me skeptically.

"He is rather attractive isn't he?" she asked assuming this is why I asked.

"Just about everyone here is attractive, but I was wondering why he was by himself. Everyone else here seems to be having a good time. The centaurs didn't look happy but they also didn't stay very long." I didn't feel the need to add that he just kept staring at me, one because I didn't want her to know that was my motive and two if she was paying attention she would see that.

"Oh" she sounded surprised. "That is Kethael; he has always been a little peculiar, especially for an elf, considering he is a high elf. For a while people thought he was a little slow because almost nobody ever heard him speak. Usually the elves are friendly and cooperative in the garden. He doesn't really like very many people, but he always comes to the celebrations and sits in the corner until it's over. There were fears for a while that he might relocate to the other side of the island but he never did. Nobody knows what he needs to feel at ease or what he is looking for." she finished.

He was still staring at me, and since he obviously has taken some strange interest in me I gave a shy smile, hoping to soften his stare but it didn't have quite the effect I thought it would have. He still stared but he rose and walked gracefully toward me. I was shocked. He was even more attractive up close.

"Hello, my name is Kethael. Forgive the intrusion but I came over to welcome you to the garden. I apologize for taking so long but your attention was directed elsewhere." he had said. The look on his face made me expect a deep voice but I was wrong. It wasn't necessarily a soft voice but it was low, wispy, and monotone.

"H-Hello," I stammered "it's nice to meet you."

He smiled and it was absolutely breathtaking. It almost instantly lit up his face like someone flipping a light switch. "Would you care to dance?" he asked. After what Faylynn had told me, his request took me by surprise.

I didn't want to be rude though so I answered "Yes thank you." He held out his hand in the offer and I took it and followed him to the floor. I felt self conscious and he moved a lot more gracefully than I did "I am not a very good dancer, actually I just learned a few simple moves earlier today" I warned.

"Well then we will keep it simple." he answered. Then he very gently placed one of my hands on his shoulder and secured the other in one of his. He placed his other hand on my waist barely touching me and we moved easily and gracefully around the floor. He kept his promise and kept it simple but if people were looking at me before they were all downright staring now.

"Why do you keep to yourself?" I asked. It may have been rude but I was just as dumbfounded as everyone else that he asked me to dance since apparently he didn't like anyone.

"You will learn in your time here that some people are very opinionated, and I believe that if two people are overly opinionated then they should avoid one another, so I do." he answered. It made sense but still didn't explain why he asked me to dance.

"What if I am opinionated?" I asked. Again I was probably being rude but I really didn't want a confrontation and I know I can be opinionated and stubborn and defensive.

"You are different, even if you are opinionated than, somehow, it will prove to be useful."

"What makes you say that?" he sounded very sure and was also being cryptic, and quite frankly I had enough of people being cryptic. It always seemed everyone was trying to tell me something without telling me anything and my brain had had enough to deal with lately it didn't need to try to do more work than necessary.

"I will explain to you at another point in time but since we seem to have every pair of eyes on us at the moment I do not believe now is the appropriate time for that." he answered. Well at least he would be willing to explain it later.

The song ended and he released me almost immediately. He offered me his arm, and when I realized what he wanted and took it he led me back to the table. As we walked I suggested "I actually want to go thank Acacia for helping me get ready today so . . . ." And I dropped my hand from his arm.

"I would like to speak more with you if you don't mind, if you would like I could walk you over but if you prefer privacy I could meet you later, that is if you wish to speak with me as well?"

I wasn't sure I wanted him to be there when I tried to speak with Kynis and I am sure he didn't want to be to close to other people if he didn't like them. "I will go over and thank her and I could meet you at the table you were sitting at if you want" I answered.

He looked relieved, whether it was because I agreed to meet back with him or because he didn't have to go talk to other people I am not sure, but either way he said "Alright I will meet you there." then he turned for the table and sat down fluidly and started sipping his wine.

I walked over to Acacia who was still talking to Kynis. "Acacia, thank you for everything and tell the girls thank you too. I love the dress and haven't had a single problem all night." I said keeping up the pretense of why I came over here.

91

"I am glad you like it, I see the dancing tips are paying off as well" she smiled superiorly at me.

"Yes, you were right, thank you for that as well. But I still say the dress is the better achievement of the two"

Well you should thank Emerenta and Glykera for that, oh and of course Kynis for the material" then she did what I was hoping she would she turned to Kynis and introduced us "Kynis this is Jenelle, Jenelle, Kynis" She said gesturing towards him.

"Of course, thank you for the material. It is fantastic and extremely comfortable."

"You are very welcome, and it's a pleasure to meet you. I knew your mother well, it was heartbreaking when she left and then passed." he said this in the same way others had mentioned her but I could hear the underlining meaning in it. Maybe that was because I had read the letters and journal.

"I wish she could be here with me. I think this would be a lot easier if I had someone close to share it with." I answered. As we talked, there was a look of shock that continued to flash in his face. I am not sure if it is because I look so much like my mother or the subtle things that make me resemble him. I wonder if he has pieced things together yet.

"Well, I just wanted to come over and say thank you." I said disappointed that my conversation with Kynis hadn't lasted longer but I couldn't think of anything else to say. Somehow saying 'I think I am your daughter' seemed a little blunt and not an appropriate topic with others around.

Just as I was about to turn and walk back to Kethael I heard Arhea make an announcement, "And now before the celebration comes to a close, the surprise I promised for the double celebration" She turned and then all of a sudden there were a couple of loud booms, fire works lit the sky and in fire above the fireworks it said Welcome Jenelle. It was beautiful except for the figure flying back down to the ground that looked like it could have been a dragon. I am sure this is exactly right, but it was still an eerie thought. Everyone cheered and then started to leave some waved at me as they left and other walked by with parting line and wishes to see me soon. There were a few who left without saying anything to me at all.

When I turned back around Kethael was still sitting at the table starring at me. I walked towards him and when I got there I just waited. I wasn't sure what he wanted to do, but considering there were still a few lingering guests I didn't think he would want to talk here.

"Would you like me to walk you home?" he asked.

"If you want"

He stood and waited for me to lead the way. He walked next to me and as soon as we were out of the square started asking me questions. "What did you do in the outside world?" he asked

"Survived." I didn't feel like going into the full length story but he wasn't going to let it go.

"And how did you do that?"

"I worked at a nursery for plants, kept food on the table, did my schoolwork, kept the house clean and avoided anything and anyone that could hurt my chances of leaving the horrible part of town that I lived in" I explained.

"Then you ended up here?' he said it like a question.

"Yes, and that was a shock all in itself, it still is sometimes. I know I have to be making all kinds of mistakes, especially when I am taken by surprise. I try not to be rude but I always feel I am when it's too late to do anything about it. I don't speak the same as some of the people here and I view things differently. I spent half my life not trusting anything or anyone and then I come here where people seem to trust everyone and everything."

"You are wrong about a few things. Actually several people don't trust one another, they just don't show it. Not everyone here gets along which I am sure you will soon see. I do not find you rude in any way. I think it is better for people to say what is on their mind instead of hiding or lying. To me a lie is rude." He said.

We were at my door now. He stood there and waited a moment. So I asked "What did you mean earlier about me being useful or something like that?"

"Well that is a rather long story but I will explain to you another time when it is not so late." he said. I should have known he would be evasive, everyone here was. But then he added "Would you like to take a walk with me tomorrow night?"

Was he really asking me on a date? This is how Kynis started dating my mother. Maybe that is how they did it here. I had never been on a date so I was a little embarrassed that he asked. I flushed and said "Ummm . . . sure . . . I guess. What time?"

"I will be here by the time the sun touches the tops of the tallest trees" he answered then he turned and left.

I went inside and planned to get undressed and fall into bed. I was exhausted. I hadn't even made to the door to my room when there was a light knock on the door. Ugh who could it be?

I answered the door and was surprised to see who was standing there. It was Kynis.

"Am I imagining things?" he asked

"What are you talking about?" I was too tired to try and be polite, even to him.

"You look very much like your mother, but you also look like . . . ." he couldn't finish his thought.

"I was wondering if you pieced that together. Would you like to come in and I will show you what I know?" I asked.

He walked in the room and looked around. The house seemed to make him sad. I remembered the last time he was in this house he was with my mother.

"How much do you know?' he asked.

"Only what I read. I found these." I said handing him the letters and my mother's journal.

He looked at the letters briefly then set them down. I didn't figure he would need to read those since he wrote them. Then he started to read my mothers journal. By the time he got to the end he looked up to me in shock and there was another look on his face.

"So you are my daughter?' he asked.

"So it would seem. Only there is apparently no way to find out for sure since my mother was the only one who knew." I said.

"Well there is another way but let me see what I can do first. I will keep in contact. Then he hugged me, which made me freeze. People didn't touch me usually. The dancing tonight was excessive to me.

He left without saying anything else. Now I was spent. I went to the bedroom, exhausted and overwhelmed. I barely managed to get the shoes off before I had collapsed in bed. Still in the dress I fell asleep on top of the sheets and blankets.

CHAPTER 9
LESSONS

When I woke up the sun hadn't even cleared the horizon. It was still a dull grey outside. I lay in bed for a few minutes thinking over the last few days. Everything in my life has been turned upside down. Even what I thought I knew about myself has been altered. I still haven't figured out exactly who or what I am. Part of me wants to just figure it all out now and get it over with, but the other part of me is worried. I have no idea how far back the cross breeding goes in my family, or on how many different levels it goes. Hopefully I will be able to get some sort of pattern down in my life. That might make the rest of it seem a little easier to deal with. I don't think that will happen for a while though. I also don't know how much more I can handle. I may need a break soon. I do start my lessons today though and that should be interesting.

As the sky started to lighten outside I decided to get ready. I decided to take a shower and wash off the makeup first. Afterwards I got dressed in a pair of jeans and a t-shirt. It was nice to wear my own clothes, especially after a night of wearing a very fancy dress. I brushed my hair and teeth. I went to the kitchen and found a bowl of strawberries. I ate a couple of those, then went and rinsed my mouth so I didn't have strawberries in my teeth all day.

The sun still hadn't entirely cleared the horizon but it was visible so I decided to head out. I didn't want to feel rushed on my way to the willow tree.

I opened my door and squealed in surprise.

"Hello Jen, Arhea sent me over to bring you a few of the things you will need for you lessons today." Alalia was saying as soon as the door started to open. She was holding what looked like a book bag but made out of leaves and silk.

"Jeez, you scared me" I said. "Thank you" I added as I took the bag from her. I looked inside and there were books and ink and what looked like porcupine quills. I guess the pen I found wasn't a normal thing in the garden. I decided to grab it just in case.

"Have a nice day." Alalia said as I walked out and started to leave. She headed in the opposite direction.

The walk to the willow tree was uneventful but enjoyable. I still couldn't believe how beautiful everything was here, and how everything seemed to be cooperative and bend or move in whatever way was needed. If I moved a branch out of the way it stayed out of the way, only snapping back when I was clear.

As I reached the willow tree Arhea came out to greet me. "You're early, what would you like to get started with first?" she asked.

"Well I was wondering what all this was for?" I asked holding up the bag.

"The books are filled with the information you will find useful, I had them copied for you last night. One of the books is actually empty. It is for you to put down anything extra that you feel you will need." she explained.

"Ok, what do you think we should start with" I asked. I had no idea what lessons there were in the garden so I didn't know where to start.

"Would you like to get history out of the way? I think a lot of the other subjects will be easier to understand when you fully appreciate the origins of the practice itself." she suggested.

"Okay, that sounds best."

She walked in the willow and I followed. She sat at the table where we had lunch the first day. I sat down and waited. "Pull out the history book and the blank book so we can get started. Don't forget your quill and ink." She said.

I pulled out the books but grabbed my pen instead of the ink and quills. She gasped. "Where did you get that?" she asked.

"I found it in my mothers stuff." I answered confused by her reaction.

"Usually only the witches and wizards have those. They travel more to the outside world then the rest of us because they can blend in better. The only others who blend as easily are of course the fae, but generally they only go once if at all." She explained. I wonder if she knew about my mother and Kynis. "You may use this if you are more comfortable with it of course." she added.

"Ok thanks."

Then we started in on the history of the garden. I paid close attention and took notes often.

"The garden was founded almost fourteen hundred years ago. It was an ideal location out of reach of unsuitable beings, and we had magic protect it from any who may accidentally stumble across it. Nobody who is unwanted can ever find this island. As people started to fall from a path from nature and its original beauty and lose any respect for not only nature but the magic of so many we decided it was time to separate from them permanently. Those who were subjected to the abuse in the outside world were invited to join us. Only those who were fit. Even the darker creatures were banned at the time. It was a paradise for those who deserved it."

"When Alicia got the other half of the island she started to allow those darker creatures and there wasn't much I could do about it except ban them from this half of the island. There have been a few points in time when we thought there would be trouble but it has always been minor."

I rarely interrupted accept when we got to the vague explanation about the other side of the island.

"How did Alicia get the other side of the island?" I asked.

Reluctantly she answered, "Originally Alicia and I shared the entire island. One day she wanted to eliminate any that we did not find suitable for the island and spread throughout the entire outside world. As for me, even if I did not find someone fit to be on the island did not mean I believed they were not fit to live. After several disagreements we decided to part ways, we split the island and lost our long standing friendship."

"And what about the darker creatures and the threat they may pose? Could there be more trouble from them?" I asked

"I am sure the threat of trouble will remain as long as they do but the time will come where it will be ended one way or the other." She ended with a tone of regret that showed she was not fond of how it would end but also one that closed the case . . . . for now.

I regretted asking, but she did not dwell on this fact. She continued into the history from that point on, giving long details about when certain species came to join them on the island. She explained the powers of fairies, nymphs, elementals, and fae.

"Fairies have many powers. They have influence over animals, in which they can get the animals to obey them under any circumstance. If they need protection or something large carried they can get an animal to do it for them. They communicate very well with animals as well. There is not an animal alive that they cannot communicate with. They also do extremely well with plants. Plants grow without question, even under harsh conditions. If a flower is having difficulties blooming a faery can aide it. It's an art of persuasion. They also are able to use the elements. Earth, air, water and fire. They use each as circumstance calls for."

"Nymphs have power over plants. The difference is they specialize in certain plants. Some nymphs have a way with trees, others are flowers or bushes. The true difference lies in the fact that nymphs can actually become one with the plant they specialize in."

"Elementals specialize in the elements. An elemental only associates with one element. Earth, air, fire, or water. They possess the ability to manipulate this element as well as possess the qualities of this element."

"Fae are unique creatures. They are actually humans who possess some fairy magic. A fae's magic isn't quite as potent as a faerie but they still can communicate with plants and animals."

"All of them have extended life spans. They will grow and a regular pace until they reach full physical maturity, after that the aging process slows to an undetectable pace that varies between species."

"We will go into the powers of other species another day. I want you to understand, so I don't want you to confuse them. These three have the most similar powers." She explained.

Then she got to cross breeding. The way she talked about it made it sound like she was indifferent. She didn't sound like she cared either way, but this was a subject I wanted to learn about in full detail.

"The very first to cross were a male fae and a nymph. It happened just a couple hundred years after the island was founded. I was astonished to find that they could cross. Shortly after word of her pregnancy spread, there was an uproar. Some creatures thought it was horrifying. Two species crossing was sure to make an abomination. When this proved to be false after the child was born, most people ended up on one side or the other. The opposing sides were those who found nothing wrong with this scenario, and those who thought it was unethical to cross breed. Still to this day there are those who, if and when two species cross, are judgmental. The centaurs are especially against it. Once several years ago there was a centaur that crossed with Pegasus. He was shunned by the entire centaur community, until one day he convinced a wizard to take away the human half of his form. He lived as a full horse until the day he died. Since he transformed into a normal creature he lost his extended life span. It was a sacrifice of love."

"Why are the centaurs so against it?" I asked

"The centaurs are highly opinionated creatures. They see things a certain way, and nothing can change their minds. It is one of their less desirable traits, I will admit. But they prove themselves time and time again especially when we need protection. They are defenders by nature." she defended. "But we will go more into centaur nature when we get to them." she concluded.

I didn't want to let the cross breeding conversation end but I guess I had no choice because she then said "That is all for history today. I think we should move on to plants. Since this will be one of your areas of expertise."

We started in on different plants. The first was the easiest, food. We had the list of plants that were grown in the harvest. How long each took, what they needed to thrive, and the best way to harvest them. "If you choose to help prepare the food we can arrange for a cooking lesson on how best to prepare different foods." She said.

After edible plants we moved to other uses for plants. "Potion making is reserved for mainly the witches but some of the other creatures help gather materials since if the plant gives them willingly instead of the ingredients being taken with force the ingredients are more potent. If you wish a course on ingredients for potions please let me know and that can also be arranged." She also explained where to get colors for dye or paint; materials for furniture, houses, or other structures; when to look for some plants for certain needs based on if they don't like too much sun or the cold. I felt like I was writing non-stop and my hand started cramping.

Finally we had covered every plant in the garden. I still wasn't sure I could recall them all off hand but I would get to them when I needed them. It was lunch time so we stopped. She prepared lunch for us; I cleared my stuff off the table so we could eat. As we were seated eating Arhea started conversation.

"Alright what do you think your time will be most useful doing? You can do anything you wish even if it is nothing at all." she asked.

"Well I guess I don't know what that would be yet. I want to focus on learning as much as I can first. I guess specializing in what I am?" I said it as a question without meaning to. I couldn't help it though considering I didn't know what I was. Arhea heard the question though and gave me a suspicious look.

"I see . . . let me ask . . . . what do you know?" she said. I still think she was trying not to overwhelm me.

I deliberated on what all to tell her. I was worried about Kynis mainly. "Anything I tell you cannot leave here until I am sure what is or isn't." I started off saying.

"As you wish" she responded surprised by my request and intensity.

"I found my mother's old journal, and read it. It said that our family line was prone to cross breeding, but didn't say with what species. I have been able to pick up the possibilities but nobody has ever told me any fact except . . ." I faltered. I was really worried about Kynis and whether or not I should say anything.

"Go on dear one." Arhea encouraged.

"Okay, so my mother had a secret relationship with Kynis and I am fairly certain that Kynis is my father not the man that raised me." I admitted.

"Oh my, does Kynis know?" she asked

"He didn't until last night." I admitted.

"Your mother was always so upset by some of the reactions to cross breeding; she was determined to end it in the family line. I guess when she fell to her emotions she was ashamed. That would explain her rush to see the outside world and her refusal to return when she got sick." she said in a sad voice.

"Why would it matter if I am a cross breed." I asked.

"Like I said there are still those who are opposed to it" she answered

"Okay, what am I crossed with?" I finally asked. I braced myself, ready for just about anything . . . . except for her response.

"I think the better question to ask is what you are not crossed with." she answered.

My jaw dropped, I could feel the blood drain from my face, a lump rose in my throat, and my chest felt tight.

She continued with "And the answer to that I am not sure, and if you are correct and Kynis is your father it is even more difficult to say since Kynis' family line is just as fluent as yours with cross breeding. And wizards throw in all sorts of extra magic in those scenarios."

"I . . . . I . . . . there . . . . " I tried to form a question but I just spluttered. Arhea tried to comfort me but nothing registered really. Only the effort but anything she said was a blur. It took me a very long time to get my grip back and breathing normal.

Finally I was able to register what Arhea was saying "It's not a bad thing, you are probably the most special creature I have in the garden. The abilities you may have are unseen in number. Our goal should be to try and find all of your abilities and teach you to use them all effectively."

"Ha . . . . So I am a freak in a place where most of the creatures are thought to not even exist. I was raised in the outside world with no guidance and now you want me to figure out what I can do and you can't even tell me what I am?" I was so filled with multiple emotions it was more overwhelming than everything combined since I came to the garden. I was mad, scared, hurt, shocked, and confused. I guess I got what I wanted though, my stupid answers!!! I am not even sure why it was upsetting me so bad.

"I can trace all you are mixed with if that will make you feel better but it will take me a few days to get it all linked together." she was still trying to comfort me after I yelled at her. All this did though was add guilt to my list of emotions. "Why don't we end our lessons for the day? We can get back to it at a later date." she suggested.

At some point I hadn't realized I started crying, so I nodded and shook tears all over myself and the table.

She rose, helped me up and walked me out of the willow tree. At some point through this I guess she realized I wouldn't be able to walk home in this state. "I will walk you home."

It took longer than it should have to get me home. The entire walk I was trembling with tears. The tears were so thick I couldn't see, my breathing was rapid, and my legs felt like jelly. Arhea had to basically carry me the entire way but tried to let me walk a little on my own. I managed to trip on everything and nothing. I couldn't come to terms with the fact that I was the ultimate mix. This couldn't be worse in a place where most people hated cross breeds.

We finally got to my house. She let us in and set me on the bench to the table. I slumped forward and laid my head on the table. I couldn't get a grip. She stayed for a while and just ran her hand along my hair. It was comforting. After what seemed like forever I finally cried myself out. I just sat there not saying a word starring at nothing. It was silent for a long time. Finally Arhea interrupted the silence. "I am sorry for your anguish. I wish there was more I could do. I will spend time this weekend finding out the information you want. We will resume lessons after the weekend. I try to use my daylight to tend to some other things on the weekends. I have to go now and see to some things before the sun sets. Will you be alright?" she asked.

I just nodded.

She left with a look of concern. I continued to sit there but I wasn't crying anymore. Occasionally my breathing would stutter after crying for who knows how long but other than that there was nothing but silence in my house. The only thing I could think of to explain why this upset me so bad was what I had thought this morning. My mind needed a break before this and this was the grain of sand that tipped the scale. It was too much and I just snapped.

Suddenly there was a knock at the door that made me jump and squeal.

CHAPTER 10

FORETELLING

I got up stiff from sitting frozen in my thoughts to answer the door. I was just starting to calm down and come to grip with things. I opened the door and realized I had forgotten that I had plans tonight.

"Good evening Jenelle, I know I am a little early but was wondering if you were ready to go?" Kethael had asked.

I wasn't sure if I wanted to go on the walk anymore. He was supposed to tell me what he meant last night about me proving to be useful. After my day I wasn't sure my brain could handle anymore, but then I thought it was best to get it all over with. I didn't want to have a surprise that set me over the edge everyday. I was probably going to regret this.

"Um . . . actually I'm not ready yet, sorry. But you can wait here for a minute while I get ready real quick." I answered.

"I will wait out here, please join me when you are ready." He answered. I was actually going to let him in the house but was glad he wanted to wait outside. I needed a few minutes to pull myself together.

"Ok, just give me a few minutes." He smiled and I shut the door.

First I went to the bedroom and picked out some clean clothes. I ended up grabbing another sun dress and my pair of sandals. I went to the bathroom and washed my face. My face was almost back to normal except a little splotchiness but you couldn't tell I was crying for a very long time. I ran my fingers through my hair trying to get it to lay flat. I looked at myself in the mirror. I realized no matter what has happened since I got here I would still have a few core traits. I remembered Arhea saying the centaurs had some less desirable traits. I also had some traits that could prove useful but weren't always nice. I was stubborn; when I set my mind there was little that could change it. I was defensive, this could sometimes cause unnecessary fights but it kept me alive. Then there were my better traits in my opinion. I am independent. I can survive. All of this made me realize that no matter what I am, what I have been told, or what I might be told tonight or ever, nothing could change who I am. All I need to figure out is what I am.

With this I felt better than I had in a couple of days. I was ready to go so I went out to meet Kethael.

"Sorry about that. I'm ready now." I said as I was closing the door behind me.

"Shall we" was his response. He turned to walk towards the forest in a new direction I have never been. I started to wonder how big the island was, considering I still hadn't been able to see the ocean.

We walked in silence for a while. I wasn't sure what he was waiting for. And I had no clue where to start the conversation. I wasn't sure I wanted to know just yet why I will be useful. We walked until the sun started to set below the tree before he said anything.

"How has your time in the garden been?" he asked making small talk.

"Well . . . ." I laughed a half-cynical laugh "After the initial shock of waking up here, it has been interesting. At first I thought I was either dreaming or dead. I didn't believe this place was real. Then I was suspicious. I haven't been in a position to trust almost anyone since my mom died so everything that was said led me to believe I was getting half truths or down right lies. Some of the things people said sounded like they were evading topics. I was caught by surprise and reacted in ways that were rude, and then sometimes I was so surprised that I literally lost my breath. I have found out things that I never believed in or even knew about to not believe in them and the amount of things I have found out about myself has been a little overwhelming."

"What sort of things have you found about yourself?" he asked with honest curiosity.

"Well the main thing is that until I got to the garden, I thought I was pure human, partly because I never thought myself to be special, and also because I didn't know there was another choice."

"I see." he said "Well you are wrong on both accounts."

We walked in silence for a little while longer. His last comment made me feel a little awkward. I wasn't sure what to think about it. I think he meant it as a compliment but so far just about everything I think here is wrong.

"Do you know all of the types of creatures that live in the garden?' he asked suddenly.

"Not all," I answered, "I have been told a few but they have been in clips or generalizations."

"Well it would be beneficial for you to know that just about everything lives here. Even some normal animals. The exception is pure humans. They are easily tainted and we do not want our paradise to be corrupted." he explained.

"How big is the island?" I asked. This might give me an idea of how many animals there are.

"Well I am not sure exactly but it is extremely large. The garden itself is grand in size and that is only half the island." he answered.

"Okay . . . ." I wasn't sure what else to say.

"In part of the forest there is and old witch who is blind. She is unable to see the present but makes up for it by seeing glimpses of the future. She goes by many names but most just call her 'Seer' for she is known by what she sees." he explained, it seemed he was getting to his point.

"And this seer saw me?" I asked assuming this is what he meant.

"Yes, it is why so many people have expectations of you. The foretelling is vague because the future is based on things following a certain path. Any choice you make, or do not make can alter the foretelling and how it will play out. If you choose to take the role fate has provided for you then the foretelling will go on with out any altercation." he explained. This actually cleared up a lot. I started thinking about the strange way people looked at me. I figured out the centaurs dislike for me when I learned they hated cross breeding, but everyone else always looked at me in a very different strange way.

"Ok and what is the foretelling?" I asked.

"I will not tell you the entire foretelling, I feel you should hear it from the seer so there is no misunderstanding what is expected of you, but part of the foretelling included me. That I will tell you." he said

I stopped walking and started fidgeting. I wasn't sure what to expect, and after not knowing what to expect for days it was starting to make me feel a little unbalanced.

"What about you?" I asked hesitantly.

"The seer sought me out to tell me that I needed to change a few habits. You see I found several hundred years ago that I did not get along very well with others. I kept to myself almost entirely, only interacting with others when it proved absolutely necessary. Seeing how this didn't happen often I was all but forgotten, and this is how I preferred it." he started telling his story. "One night I was sitting at home when there was a knock on my door. This surprised me, not very many outside of Arhea knew where I lived and Arhea respected my desire for privacy. She had only been to my home once and that was when I wanted approval to live there." He walked a little ways more before he leaned against a tree to continue his story. I sat on a rock a little ways in front of his tree. "With my preferred seclusion, I also lacked familiarity with others in the garden so I knew nothing of the seer, or her reputation. I was surprised to see an old, blind witch at my doorstep. At first I assumed she was lost and offered to direct her to another course. I tried not to be rude, of course but was irritated that someone stumbled across my location." He half smirked.

"Then the seer said 'do not alter my path Kethael, for I am here to deliver a message of grave importance to you and you would be wise to listen'. I was shocked that the blind witch knew not only my name but that it was me she was talking to. She explained that she was born without sight of the present, but she had been able to see glimpses of the future since she could remember. She said that throughout time she had been piecing together an event. It had come in flashes, and took several years to connect the facts, since each decision could change any individual part of the future or shift it completely. She then said that I played a part in this future of the utmost importance."

He had paused so I asked "what was your part, and what does it have to do with me?"

"The seer said '*I can not see exactly when but a newcomer will join the garden. She will be destined to be here, as her family has been here for generations. She will have been raised in the outside world and will need guidance by several, but you must be part of the elite team who will help her fulfill her destiny.*' I asked her what destiny and why must I be part of this team. She said that I must be part of the team because not only will I prove most useful to this newcomer but she will prove useful to me as well. She then told me the rest of the foretelling but as I said before I will not tell you that part. I think the seer should tell you that personally." he said

"Where is the seer? How am I supposed to find her?" I asked.

"She lives beyond the village. There are few that live over there, and even less live in houses, so it should be easy enough to find when you go to look for it."

"Ok . . . . so . . . . is that all then?" The foretelling had me worried about one of my original fears. What could these people expect of me? I also remember Arhea telling me she was going to ease me into this, and I guess it was good if that's what happened. A few days is a hard time to wrap my head around this world but apparently enough time because if I was told this on my first day I probably would have turned around and went home.

"What do you mean?" he asked.

"Well the reason you wanted to go on this walk was to tell me why I was useful wasn't it?"

"Not necessarily." he answered "I chose to tell you on this walk because we would be out far enough that nobody could hear. Like I said not everyone here trusts one another. Well I am one of those who don't trust any of them, and I have yet to be given a reason to trust them."

"So . . . you don't trust me?"

"No, I am unsure why, but from the moment I saw you at the celebration last night I felt I could trust you."

I couldn't help feeling awkward again. "So then why did you want to go on this walk?"

"I wanted to spend time with you. I haven't trusted anyone for a much longer time than you; I wanted to enjoy the company of someone I trusted. Although I chose my solitude I do get lonely." he explained.

"Ok . . . . so what do you want to talk about?" I asked. I knew what it felt like to choose to avoid those around you but still be lonely.

"I would like to find out how we could be useful to one another, for starters, and if you don't want to discuss that then whatever you wish."

"Actually I think that's a really good idea. I was sort of wondering about that anyway."

"So what are your thoughts?"

"Your guess is better than mine. I am still new at this whole place, remember?"

"Yes, I remember. Well do you know what your abilities are?"

"Not really, I know I have a way with plants and that I can hear unicorns, but that's basically all I got so far. I just started my lessons today."

"You can hear unicorns?" he asked. "That is interesting."

"Why is that so interesting, apparently there are a few people in my family who could or can?"

"What are you?" he asked.

"Ummm . . . I don't know entirely. I am basically the ultimate cross breed. I found out today. Arhea is supposed to figure it out for me and get back to me."

He just stared at me, nothing to say. It made me uncomfortable and I was worried that he was one of those who disliked cross breeds.

"Is something wrong?" I asked.

"No I just thought that an ultimate cross breed wouldn't look so human."

"Well I don't think I have any centaur in me." I said.

He laughed and said "No I guess you wouldn't. I have only heard of one centaur cross breed. The centaur responsible for the cross had a very unfortunate fate. I would think his story serves as a warning to other centaurs."

"Yea, I heard about that. I guess you're right though, it could be seen as a warning."

"So I guess we will have to find out more about you to figure out how you will be useful to me, and I think this is one way I can prove to be useful to you. I will help you find what your abilities are and also help uncover any information you need, if I can."

"How do we find out what I can do?" I asked.

"Well, first, I think its best to find out what you are, so we know where to start."

"Arhea said it's a better question to ask what I am not." I said morosely. But to my surprise Kethael laughed. "What's so funny?" I demanded getting defensive.

"Why do you look so upset to be so unique? People and creatures alike try to be different in some way, better, and here you are possibly the best of them all, and you look miserable at the thought." he answered still chortling to himself.

"How does being different make me possibly the best of them all?" I asked, still irritated.

"Well, lets consider the possibilities of your genetics shall we, If you are mixed with all of them then you have the potential to do what any of them can do plus so much more. If you are informed, trained, and practiced you could very well be the most powerful thing here. Even more than the dragons." He said. The look on his face was one of awe and it just irritated me more in my already aggravated state.

"Stop looking at me like that. For all we know I could be the ultimate fluke and barely maintain the fae qualities in me." I snapped.

He tried to make his expression change but he ended up switching to one of intensity, "Why must you berate yourself like that?" He asked. "I have never met anyone like you. I find you entertaining and charming even when you are upset with me. You should never doubt yourself. I am sure you will see, and you will show not only yourself but everyone else just how special you are."

I sat fuming for a while. Although it made me feel a little self conscious, the fact that he seemed sincere in his complimenting made me feel a little better. I was sure I acted like a fool.

"I'm sorry I got mad at you." I said quietly.

"Ah, well we will just assume that if you have a little of all the creatures then it includes dragons. So we will blame it on the heat boiling underneath your human appearance." he laughed. And to my surprise this made me feel better too, and I joined in his laughter.

"It's getting late, and I have had a long day, so let's save the rest of this conversation for later. Hopefully we will have more information to work with then." I said smiling.

"As you wish, let's head back." he agreed.

He walked me back to my house in silence just as he was on our way to the location we had stopped. It wasn't until we were outside my door that he said anything else.

"You know, you may prove to more than just useful to me." he said. "At the very least you may be a true friend."

I smiled at that thought. "Thank you, I'm glad you feel that way." I really wanted true friends, and if this seer said we could be useful to each other, I couldn't think of a better way than to have a real friend to confide in.

His next comment took me completely off guard. A friend was great, and he seemed to except me for who I am and even like it. I was still trying to figure out who I was and wasn't really looking past that too far.

He said "And just so you are informed, I am not against cross breeding." He said quietly, and then added "I will come visit you in the next few days and we can have another talk if you have the time. Have a pleasant night Jenelle." and he turned and disappeared in the trees.

It took me a minute to unfreeze my shocked frame. I wasn't sure if he was just telling me he accepted me or if he was implying something else. The tone in his voice and the look on his face made me think it was the latter.

This was just something I couldn't think about now. I had enough to deal with already. I was finally able to get in my house. I ate a quick snack, brushed my teeth, changed my clothes, and went to bed.

The day of learning, crying, and walking had worn me out completely. I hadn't felt this tired in a long time. Even yesterday didn't feel this bad. I fell into another troubled sleep.

CHAPTER 11

FAMILY

I guess my life is taking a new routine that I hadn't quite realized. I wake up, get ready, try to follow a plan, and get a new shock or surprise, then come home and try to get sleep with all the excess information flying around in my head. Maybe I should stop trying to make a plan. Maybe some of the information won't come as such a shock and I won't react like I did yesterday.

I got up and started to get ready. I moved slowly today, getting ready at a leisurely place. I wasn't on a time limit to be anywhere and it felt good to take my time. Walking around the house putting things up, cleaning what little mess there was, made me feel a little more like myself. While I did that I was thinking about my idea to stop making definite plans or expectations so I wouldn't be able to be as shocked. I had finally come to a full resolve that I would try to do whatever made me happy here, since there really wasn't a need to do anything.

So with my new resolve of expecting a surprise I tried to figure who I wanted to see today. Kethael said he would come see me over the next few days so I guess I will see him whenever he shows up. Arhea said she would be busy. I don't know where to find Alalia, Kynis, or Emerenta. So that leaves Faylynn.

I headed to the square. I wasn't sure which house was Faylynn's but I was sure I could ask someone one. When I got there I found out that it wasn't necessary. Faylynn was outside her house.

"How are you today Fay . . . ." her look had me backtracking, "I mean . . . grandma?" I asked.

"Good, and you?"

"I'm good."

"What can I help you with today?" she asked as I reached her front door.

"Well mostly I just came for a visit. I was wondering about my family, the only family I knew in the outside world were my parents so . . ."

"Oh," she looked surprised "I hadn't thought of that actually, I am so sorry. Why don't you come in and we can talk, and I will tell you as much as I can."

I followed her into the house. It was set up a lot like mine except hers was a little bigger. I assume this is because she had children here at some point. She gestured for me to sit on the couch while she went to the bookshelf. She pulled down several books. When she sat down next to me I realized they were large picture albums.

"So in your time here in the garden I assume you have heard the reputation of our family?" she asked.

"Yea, a couple times." I answered half laughing.

"That doesn't surprise me, and from the sound of your voice I am guessing that you have already figured out most peoples views on the matter."

"Yea, but I seem to have talked to only those who don't mind cross breeding." I answered.

"Well that's good. So what do you want to know?" she asked.

"Well, I actually have Arhea doing a full background on everything I am mixed with; mostly I want to know my living relatives. I never really had a family, outside of my mom I never saw anyone that was even on my . . . . *fathers* family." I couldn't help saying father through gritted teeth; maybe I should just call him by his name.

"I have heard some not pleasant things about him, do you want to talk about it?" she asked with concern.

"Not really, after my mom died, David turned to drugs, alcohol, and sketchy women. There really isn't much to talk about." I answered dully. Calling him by his name was much better.

"Okay dear," she still had the note of sadness in her voice but she tried to perk it up when she obviously changed the topic "So living relatives it is then." She then started flipping through the books and taking out pictures. After she was done she sorted them and started with my aunts and uncles.

Throughout the course of the morning I learned that Faylynn had 3 daughters total. My mother was the youngest and out of her two older sisters, Clairette and Evvie, Evvie was married to a fae named Cyril and they had two children, Brax and Nysha and Clairette lived alone in a house outside of the village. Clairette was like Kethael in the fact that she didn't associate with others if it was avoidable.

Fayette had a sister but I never got an explanation on where she was or her name. When we got to her picture Faylynn had said "Oh, that's my sister . . . ." she switched the picture almost immediately and I only got a glance of it "and this is a picture of me and my late husband" and I saw a picture of what I am assuming was their wedding. He almost looked like he could be

120

Fae except the picture was blurry. Either he moved or he was an elemental. After all was said and done and we had gone through the few pictures there were she asked "Any questions dear?"

"Will I ever get to meet Clairette and Evvie?" I asked.

"Yes I am sure you will, Evvie and her family are busy today and Clairette will be difficult to get a hold of if she doesn't want to be, but in time." she answered. I didn't ask about her sister because I could sense she was uncomfortable talking about her. I would find out eventually why. She then changed the subject; I think she was worried I was going ask about her sister. "So how about some lunch?" she asked.

"Okay."

We went into her dining area and she made us lunch. While we ate she made mild conversation about what I had been doing since she last talked to me. I only told her about my lessons. I didn't want to tell her about Kethael or the foretelling.

After we had finished eating, I realized that, although I was happy that I finally had a family, my life of avoiding interaction made long visits uncomfortable.

"I think I am going to head home, I wanted to read some more of my books before my lessons start back up next week." I said, giving myself an excuse to leave without being rude.

"Alright Jen, just come back and visit me whenever you want" she said with a smile. She walked me out and saw me off. From what I could tell she stood there until I was out of sight.

When I made it home I had another surprising visitor. Kynis was waiting for me at my front door.

"Jenelle, I am glad you are here. I have been waiting, hoping you would come home soon." he said as soon I as I was close enough o hear him.

"Hey, what's going on?" I asked.

"Can we go inside?" he asked looking around making sure nobody could hear him.

"Ok." I answered. I opened the door, walked in, and waited for him to follow.

I shut the door and turned on him. He had a mixture of excitement and worry on his face. "Okay, are you going to tell me what this is all about?" I asked.

"There are a few things, do you want to sit?" he asked pointing at the table.

We both sat down and he was a little fidgety, I wondered what he was going to tell me.

"Would you like the good news or the difficult news first?" he asked.

"Why don't we do the difficult news first?" I suggested. I was hoping the good news would counter act the difficult news. He didn't say bad news though so I was trying to take comfort in that.

"Okay so to try and figure out some things . . . . I had to go see some . . . . um . . . . less sociable people." he said still fidgeting. "Well I went and visited . . . . a witch . . . . she has a certain ability . . . . to see things." He hedged.

I instantly knew what he was talking about "The seer?" I asked.

He looked shocked that I knew about her. "Yes, how did you know of her?" he asked.

"A friend who had also spoken with the seer about me. He wouldn't tell me all of her foretelling though. He said he thought it would be best for me to hear it from her so there were no misunderstandings, but he played a small part in the foretelling and he told me about that." I answered in a very off-hand voice. If this was all the difficult part was then that was good.

"Oh, well then I suppose your friend was right about you hearing it for yourself from her. And the foretelling was the difficult part. So then, on to the good news, well at least it is good news to me." he said looking like he was about to blush.

"Great, what's the good news?" I asked.

"Turns out, you are my daughter. Biologically that is, I mean I knew you grew up knowing another as your father and if you feel like that bond is stronger, by all means, please let me know. I could be a friend or I could stay out of your life if you choose. No matter what I will respect your wishes." he babbled on. I was waiting for him to calm down or even take a breath. He even repeated himself a couple times. Then, finally, after I think he talked himself up enough and was prepared for whatever my answer was he stopped and looked at me waiting for my response.

"Well, it's a relief that the difficult news was nothing more than you thinking I was completely unaware of the foretelling. Second, as far as the good news, apparently you hadn't heard what my life was like in the outside world. It was nothing short of miserable after my mom died. The disgusting man my mother thought to be a suitable father turned to drugs, alcohol, and a variety of other disgusting habits after she died. If he got too drunk and ran out of distractions, he beat up on me. I was more than relieved to come here, and even ecstatic at the thought that I might have a different father, so it is good news, and although it may take time to be able to call you dad or anything, I am very happy and would like you in my life. From the sounds of things this foretelling is pretty serious, and I am going to need all the help I can get. Since not only are you my father but also the only wizard I know so far I may need you to help me learn my abilities." I concluded.

Kynis looked like he was about to burst with joy. I thought he might actually do a dance. He beamed and said "Of course I will help you. That would be great, and I know your mother wanted to keep our love a secret so I will leave the decision up to you whether or not you want to tell people of our relationship, or you can tell them we are friends since I was such good friends with you mother, either way." he looked so happy I could probably tell him to not even be seen in public together and it wouldn't have fazed him.

"For now lets just not say anything, I am sure people will ask eventually but we will get to that when we get there." was my answer.

"That sounds like a plan to me" he said.

"So how has your experience been here in the garden so far?" he asked. It seemed like he didn't want to leave. I didn't mind but I wanted to get some questions in before he left.

"It's been interesting at the very least. It is hard trying to wrap my mind around a life and place that I would have never imagined existed in the first place but I seem to be getting the hang of it pretty well, I think."

"Well I would assume it is very different in the outside world. I went once, long after your mother died, it was only for a couple of hours but I wanted to see the things she saw, but found the people there were rude and pushy so decided to let others go for me if I needed anything."

"What stuff do you get there? Arhea said that the wizards go, but didn't tell me why."

"Some of the things in the garden were hard to come by on an island. We did need protein and the plants didn't suffice so we went and got some animals for food. We couldn't fathom turning on each other for meals. Then there are things we use in our work. Plus there are some things that are just nice to have. Cameras, pens, paper, and other novelties like that." he answered.

We talked about different things, mostly surrounding wizards. Eventually I got out my notebook and started writing notes down.

"What are you doing?" he asked when I first grabbed it.

"I am keeping track of anything that might become useful later. It is a lot to take in and since I am taking so much in such a short time I am trying to write as much down to keep my thoughts organized." I answered.

"That is very intelligent of you." he commented. Then we returned to our conversation. We talked about the work wizards do and that most don't actually meet their potential because they stick to simple concoctions to benefit the garden. Very few practice their magic in higher fields. We talked for hours. I had filled almost six pages before the sun was starting to set.

"I should be off. This was an enjoyable visit. We should do this more often. If you ever want a visit I live in one of the houses at the opposing end of the village on the fringe of the forest. You will know my house when you see it, for it has some qualities the others don't." he said getting up.

"I would like to do this again and I might need more help. I will come see you soon." I answered and he beamed again. Then he gave me another hug. I guess I was going to have to get used to this if I was going to see him more.

He left, and to my surprise, I didn't have one shocking surprise today. I guess my not planning plan worked really well.

I went to bed that night and had the first good night sleep since my first night here.

———⟨⟩———

I slept in pretty late. By the time I had finally woken up fully rested and stress free the sun was almost all the way in the sky. I was guessing it was around nine. Maybe I could get Kynis to get me a clock so I would know what time it was, and also possibly a calendar.

My day today was going to be set trying to find the seer. I rummaged through the house until I found a few things that I thought could be useful. I would rather have extra things for my adventure then not enough. I gathered all the things I collected and placed them in my book bag Alalia brought me the other day. Then I set out.

I walked out of the house and headed in a straight line. Kethael said she lived on the far side of the village in an area of the forest that only outcasts go. I mildly wondered if this was where Kethael lived while I walked. As I passed the last house that still belonged to the village I started to wonder where to head first.

I continued to walk forward for a while until I could see a few breaks in the trees to both sides of me. I decided to go left first, then double back if that turned out to be a dead end. As I walked closer to the opening the air changed. It started to have a salty smell to it. I assumed I was heading to the beach.

I was almost to the opening when I heard someone approaching me. It sounded like hoofs. I wondered what it was. I turned to see who or what it was prepared for just about anything . . . . except for what I saw.

I stood frozen in place not daring to move, sure that if I did I would be dead.

CHAPTER 12

EXPLORATION

From around the side of one of the trees was a bow, arrow loaded, pointed at me? I wasn't sure what to do. This was the first openly hostile encounter I have had since I came to the garden.

A gravelly female voice come from behind the tree "Who are you? Why are you here? Answer quickly and don't move or it will be the last thing you do."

Barely moving even my lips I answered as fast as I could "My name is Jenelle, I just recently came to the garden and am looking for the seer who supposedly told a foretelling regarding my future. Nobody will tell me what it is; they all said I should hear it from her."

The torso of a woman bent around the tree, I could only see her face, chest, and the arms holding the bow. Her skin was dark, not exactly brown but the color of faded leather. Her hair was pitch black and was wavy down past her shoulders. She had on a worn black leather vest the barely covered her upper body. Her eyes were golden brown. Her expression was wary. She scrutinized me, especially my face. She lowered the bow partially but still had it ready to shoot; it was just no longer pointed at me . . . for now. "You are the being from the outside world that the seer predicted?" she asked.

"I guess so; I haven't found her yet to be sure." I answered, relieved that she has also heard of the foretelling. I assumed that this fact alone could save my life.

"You said your name was Jenelle?" she asked.

"Yes, my name is Jenelle, I am Amelinda's daughter." I answered.

"Yes, I believe that. You look like Amelinda." She said "My name is Zula." she added as she stepped around the tree.

I was instantly aware of who she was when I saw her entire body. She was a centaur, mostly. Her body was the same pitch black as her hair. Her distinguishing factor was the very large, beautiful, white wings protruding from her back. This stood in extreme contrast to her dark coloring. This was the only centaur cross breed.

"It's nice to meet you Zula. Did you know my mother?"

"Yes, she was one of the few people who ever talked to me. I am an unspeakable person, even when my tale is told I am not mentioned only my father is." she answered.

"Yeah, I heard about what happened. What about your mother?" I asked. I instantly regretted it.

Pain twisted her face and her voice when she answered "When my father died she abandoned me to rejoin the Pegasus on top of their mountain." she answered.

"That's terrible." I answered.

"Yes, so I was left banned from both worlds. I live on my own here and associate with the other outcasts as need requires." she answered. Then she changed the subject "If you are looking for the seer, why are you headed that direction?" she asked.

"I didn't know where she lived, and then I smelled the salt in the air and wanted to see the ocean." I answered.

"Well I wouldn't go to far that way."

"Why? Is there something wrong with the beach?"

"You obviously have much to learn. I will show you around this part of the garden so you understand." She started walking towards the beach and I followed.

We stopped at the edge of the trees and I could see the beach, the ocean, and a tall mountain that touched the clouds. The top of the mountain was hidden. The ocean sparkled. The sand gradually turned into the forest floor we were on.

"The ocean is not too dangerous right along the beach, but do not ever venture further then knee deep. The creatures that dwell there will take you to the depths of the ocean and you will never be seen again. The mountain is harder to explain. The top is where the Pegasus live in peace. If you are not pure of mind, body, and spirit they will not hesitate to throw you off into the ocean. The real trouble is to get to the top. If you cannot fly it is nearly impossible, for at the base of the mountain are the twins, Degalla and Defarra. They are sphinx and protect the Pegasus. Arhea placed them there and you have to be able to outsmart them to get to the mountain. Whether you know or not, it is almost impossible to outsmart their riddles. They are the brightest sphinx I have ever seen; it is why Arhea is so fond of them." She explained.

"Okay, thanks for the advice. You know you probably just saved my life. I was sure to go swimming at the very least."

"Jenelle, you must realize that there is a reason those on this section of the garden are outcasts. On the other side the only creatures you should be wary of are the centaurs but that is only because they are highly opinionated and if you offend them then there is a small chance of regaining their favor. The satyr's and pixies have a mischievous nature but are not dangerous. The wizards and witches that live over there are not likely to harm anyone either, but here it is different. You must always proceed with caution. Disrespect and foolishness can end your life. If you are the one, then you must not put yourself in harms way, and if you must then carefully. I think it would be best if I be your guide from now on. Please do not venture in this part of the forest without me." she seemed to feel very strongly about this topic.

"That is fine with me, how will I contact you if I want to come here though?" I was actually really happy to have someone watching to make sure I don't screw up.

"When you enter these parts call my name and wait until I meet you. I will be listening for your call." she answered.

"Would you show me more about this part of the garden? And please explain as much as you can."

"Of course, we will cover this then I will take you to the seer." she answered.

I pulled my book and pen out. And started writing what she told me so far. I stopped before I got too far "What is in the ocean?" I asked.

"Sea serpents mostly but there is rumor to be more. The rumors are worse than the fate the sea serpents present." she answered.

I wrote this down then continued on about the mountain and the Pegasus. I wrote everything down in as much detail as I could. I also wrote notes on what to do or not do in most cases. Knee deep or less in the water, unless you can outsmart the sphinx, don't go near base of mountain, and if you can ever make it to the top of the mountain make sure you are pure or you will be thrown in the ocean to the sea serpents or worse.

"Okay, what else?" I asked, pen in hand and waiting.

"Throughout the forest there are few, but if you should cross any one of them be careful. Most are witches or wizards who chose solitude, there is one elf, and a handful of cross breeds there are a few creatures here that fall into none of these categories. The sphinx, the Pegasus and then those in the cavern. The witches and wizards may regard you differently because of who you are but make sure to proceed with caution until they are aware. The elf will avoid anyone, at almost any cost. Until recently he was hardly ever even seen . . . ."

She was about to continue down her list of explanations when I burst out laughing "Kethael?" I asked.

"You know him by name?" she was extremely surprised "How?" she asked.

"Kethael only started to be seen because the seer found him. He has been waiting for me so he started going to the celebrations. He is supposed to be important; a part of an elite team to help me with whatever the foretelling says I am going to do." I explained.

"I, also, am to be part of that *elite* team." she answered putting a sarcastic emphasis on the word elite, still looking shocked.

"Really?" I was surprised to hear this.

"Yes, the elite team is to be made up of myself and six others. I have found out who exactly three of these others are and a brief description of the other three. I knew there was an elf, but didn't suspect Kethael because he is so isolated. There is also a wizard-nymph cross breed and fae. The three I am sure of are Arhea, Jarita, and Baellon. Baellon is to be in the lead." she explained.

"The wizard-nymph cross bred in Kynis. Who are Jarita and Baellon?" I asked.

"I am glad you knew two out of the missing three. As far as the other two go let us continue with our explanation then we will get to them." she answered.

"Okay." I went back to my book. I wrote down what she had told me about my elite team with blank spots next to the one empty spot. I still didn't know who the fae was.

"As I was saying, the cross breeds are not all friendly, they have been shunned and more or less forced into isolation. We associate with each other so that should include you once they learn who you are. That takes care of those in the forest, and then we get to the cavern."

"What's in the cavern?"

"We are almost there."

We walked for about twenty more minutes. Then there was another break visible in the trees up ahead. As we got closer I noticed another change in the air, but instead of a salty smell, it smelled like something burning. As we reached the edge of the trees Zula stopped me again so I could see but wouldn't let me go further.

"What's going on?" I asked.

"Before we go any further, you must understand. Jarita lives toward the top of the cavern. There is a small opening with a cliff in front of it. To get there will be no feat and Jarita is the only one of her kind that lives in the garden. This is good for we have no fear of being ambushed, but Jarita is powerful and if we do not enter respectfully, act cautiously and explain quickly we both could be in grave danger."

"Okay, I will follow your lead."

"That sounds like the best plan, but if we survive Jarita, then we must venture to the bottom of the cavern. Baellon is a cross breed and he is the one we want to see. His cave is the first, which makes that a little easier, and hopefully we will be in Jarita's favor and we will have a look out. However in the other caves lie the dragons. Most will ignore us but if we disturb Kalian it will be our lives."

Suddenly, I remembered I had heard Jarita's name before and it was in addition to Kalian. These were the guests complained about during the meeting on my first day. When Arhea had come back from talking to them she looked like she was rolled in a fire pit. My stomach started twisting in knots and my throat felt like it was closing. I guess the fear showed on my face.

"Do not worry Jenelle, as long as we are quick and we follow the plan we should be safe. We must hurry though." Zula urged.

She started walking and I followed her lead. The plan was good. I was to watch Zula and try to behave like she did. This was more difficult then I had planned. I hadn't taken into consideration that Zula's lower body would move differently than mine did. We both still moved quickly to the edge of the cavern, down a slope, and around a ledge, until we reached the cliff in front of a small cave. Zula stopped and so did I. She waited for a moment listening hard inside the cave. Then she looked at me with a look on her face that was difficult to read, it almost looked like fear. "I have encountered a small problem in our plan" she whispered to me. "Jarita has no human form. There is no way to know how she feels about the situation, anything more than a nod will be beyond me. We will have the same complication with Baellon. I am sorry I didn't see it before now."

I thought about this for a moment. How could we get past this problem? There had to be an answer . . . . then like a lightening bolt it hit me. I could hear animal's thoughts, at least the unicorns. Maybe I could hear Jarita and Baellon too. It had to be the answer considering they were both part of my elite team.

"Don't worry about that." I whispered back "I think I can. At least I can hear unicorn's thoughts. I don't know if it's all magical creatures but it's the only plan we have."

Zula was surprised to hear this "Hopefully you are right about this." Then she turned toward the cave opening. She held her hands very still in front of her and looked at me to mimic. I did and then she called into the cave in a very calm, quiet voice. "Jarita, my name is Zula. I have with me a guest who would like to meet you. We mean you no harm." Then she waited listening intently.

Suddenly we heard a flapping of wings, and then we saw a slight flickering in the cave. Abruptly there was a bird that looked like it was on fire. Its feathers flickered with the flames but did not seem to hurt it. We both waited. Zula eyes kept glancing at my face. Then she said "Jarita, this is Jenelle. Jenelle, Jarita."

Zula looked at me again with meaning in her eyes. "Hello Jarita. I am sorry we have disturbed you. I have come here because I have been told of a foretelling that will include an elite team of members to help me. From my understandings you are to be one of them." I said politely, trying to keep the calm, quiet in my voice like Zula had used.

135

We both waited, my heart started racing. What if I was wrong?

"Yes, the seer came a saw me quite some time ago to prepare me for this" I heard her thought and gave a great sigh.

"From my understanding so far, my entire team had been visited from the seer. We were also wondering if you would please do us a favor." I asked. I knew we had to be quick. Jarita was only a part of our concerns.

"What would that be, Jenelle?"

"We need to go to the bottom of the cavern. We must also speak with Baellon. I want to be able to meet my entire team, but also I want to make sure he is aware he is on the team."

"I fail to see the favor from me in that Jenelle."

"Please call me Jen, and the favor is while we are down trying to talk to Baellon, will you please keep watch for Kalian. From my understanding he is not forgiving when disturbed."

"I will do as you ask Jen, and please be careful. Your form does not look very tough so you will need protectors. Baellon will be more than sufficient for your needs, but is no match for those like Kalian."

"Thank you, when we return to the top, you are welcome to join us if you wish to speak more."

"We shall see, now go quickly."

I turned to Zula, who looked both confused and impressed. "I will explain more later, for now lets go. Jarita is going to keep watch.

We were even quieter trying to climb down the steeper slope to the bottom. We moved slowly so we didn't attract attention by making too much noise. Finally we reached the bottom. It felt like it took forever, but we made it.

At the bottom of the cavern there wee several large caves, some with smoke billowing out of them. Closest to us was one that was noticeably smaller than the rest. Zula nodded towards this one. When we reached the mouth of the cave Zula put one hand out in front of me, and then nodded forward. I understood this, we were going in but we needed to use caution.

We walked into the cave slowly barely moving our legs. We were in few feet before Zula stopped again. In a hushed voice she said "Baellon, My name is Zula. I have with me a guest that would like to meet you. We mean you no harm."

Just then there was a thudding coming form the back of the cave, followed by a burst of flame. A huge creature approached us. I knew this was a dragon. He was beautiful. His scales were a dark silvery purple, the membrane on his wings was a brilliant shade of jade that reminded me of the trees, and his eyes were sky blue.

"*Finally, I have been waiting for you. I am sure you know the seer has sought me out. Did she also tell you my job in your team?*"

"No, I actually haven't met her yet." I answered still in a hushed voice. "I heard of the foretelling from another member of my team. I am actually going to go find her when I am done here. I still need to figure out who the last person in my team is."

"*You should know I am your guardian. I was told by the seer that you would find me and from that point on I was to protect you. Do you mind if I follow you? I will not over step my bounds and I will stay a little distance from your home. I have already arranged new placement with Arhea, I was just waiting for your arrival.*"

"That's sounds good to me, I guess. I am not sure what I need protection from, but it couldn't hurt." Just as I was finishing my sentence Jarita gave a loud screech and the ground rumbled under out feet followed by a sinister growling.

"Kalian" Zula proclaimed not bothering to use her hushed voice anymore since we have been found out.

"Have her take you out of here. I will hold him off and meet you at the seer."

"Zula, he wants you to take me out of here while he holds him off. He said he will meet us at the seer." I rushed out.

"Take you out of here? He can't hide us somewhere?" she asked.

"Kalian doesn't usually leave the cavern, and he shouldn't go after you in any case because then he would have to deal with Arhea. As long as you are in the cavern though you both are in danger."

"He says if we stay we are in danger but he shouldn't follow us"

"But what about his fire breath? That can follow us." Zula protested.

"I will block you, just hurry before it's too late. If he makes it to the mouth of this cave he will block our only exit."

"He said he will block us but if we wait until he makes it to the front of the cave we will lose our only exit."

"Fine! Climb on my back, sit behind the wings and hold on to my shoulders." She ordered.

I followed instructions immediately.

CHAPTER 13

SEER

As I scrambled on the back of Zula I could hear Kalian getting closer. Jarita's screeches were getting louder but still being drowned out by the thudding of Kalian and the occasional roar he let out. When I was in place Zula yelled "HOLD ON!" and her wings spread touching either side of the cave. I was momentarily distracted from the danger at hand by the beauty of her wing span. When they were open, there wasn't as much of a contrast between her body and wings. The base of her feathers was black like her body and they slowly faded from black, to five shades of grey, until the last few feet were white.

Baellon was already heading towards the front of the cave. Zula spun and galloped toward the entrance. Her front feet were off the ground preparing for flight before we reached the opening of the cave. We could hear Baellon, Kalian, and Jarita all close. As soon as Zula was out of the cave we were rising at an incredible pace. I felt like I was going to fall backwards, causing me to tighten my grip on Zula. I felt the heat of fire behind us and risked a glance back towards the cavern. Jarita's small flames on her feathers had erupted she was now fully ablaze and circling Kalian's head. Baellon was pushing at his lower half so he was both distracted and having difficulties moving forward. Kalian was more than three times the size of Baellon, and there was no comparison for the difference between him and Jarita. Kalian was a brilliant scarlet and emanated fury and danger.

We had reached the top of the cavern but were still flying. She seemed determined to make sure we were out of harms way. When we reached the trees she started to go down. It was amazing how graceful she moved. We glided down through the trees and landed softly in the forest. I started to climb off, not wanting to stay on her back. Somehow I felt it might be degrading since she wasn't a normal horse. I moved slowly trying not to hurt her in anyway.

"Are you alright?" Zula asked when I was on the ground. She turned so she could look at me. There was concern in her face as she checked me over before I was able to give my answer.

"I'm alright." I answered. In truth I was. My heart was pounding and my breath was highly accelerated but I wasn't hurt in any way. I even felt a little triumphant.

"Good, then let's head to the seer. It will be dark before we are able to leave her house and I do not want to make our journey any later than necessary." she turned and headed into the forest. I followed her in silence.

We were deep into the forest before Zula said anything. "Do you still want to learn about this part of the forest?" she asked.

"Yes, please." I answered pulling out my book and adding information from the cavern. Then I looked at her just in time to see that she had stopped. I had almost run into her.

"This is the end of our garden." she stated. "There is a small space considered nomads land where Arhea and Alicia meet to discuss whatever it is they have to discuss. But no one is to go into the nomads land except Arhea. She is the only one who is protected. Nomads land means that you can be attacked without provocation." She was pointing towards an opening a few feet ahead. It looked like the tree line abruptly ended and

140

there was an empty space. The trees seemed to start back up a little bit further but they weren't the lush healthy trees around us, they looked dark and sinister. Like the type of trees I would see around my house in the outside world.

I wrote this down in detail, what Zula said and what everything looked like. As I finished we both looked up. There was a loud flapping above us. As we looked up we say Baellon coming down from the sky to land. He landed and looked at Zula then me.

"It's a very fair thing I am relocating. I fear I am no longer welcome in the cavern. Jarita seemed to fare better than myself, for she is also immune to fire but as you say her cavern in so small she is safe within it."

"I am sorry if I caused you any trouble. If you wanted to go back I am sure Arhea would go and have a talk with Kalian."

"Don't worry Jenelle. Kalian has never liked me. I am a disgrace for I am not a full dragon. I am much like your friend here. I am not welcome in either world of my parentage."

"You are a cross breed? What are you mixed with?" I asked. I wondered why he was so much smaller than Kalian.

"The cross in which I came to be has turned into a rumor. I unfortunately outgrew my birth mother. She was desperate you see. She wanted a powerful child and since she had not found a suitable father for her goals she convinced a wizard to impregnate her with dragon. I, as you can see, have a dragon body. Her small, fragile form couldn't hold me. Unknowingly, I slowly ripped my mother from inside out. Her womb could not handle my claws and I was too big to prevent from killing her. She died shortly after I had been expelled from her stomach. She died a painful death, slowly bleeding while her insides refused to stay where

they belonged. She named me while I sat with her, too afraid to leave her side to look for help and leave her to die alone. The compassion and understanding is not typical for a dragon, that is assumed to be proof of my alternate parentage."

"I am sorry to hear that." I really didn't know how to comfort him. He killed his mother because of her own stupidity.

"I am sorry to interrupt but we must be going." Zula said.

"Okay, let's go."

We walked a little further along the edge of the garden until we reached a small, circular clearing. On the edge of the clearing was a small wooden house. It reminded me of a log cabin.

"You should go in alone Jenelle. We will wait out here for you." Zula had said.

I walked up to the front door of the cabin. I stood there for a moment trying to prepare myself. No matter what she tells me, I must not get scared and run away. My time here has made it so I cannot abandon the garden, especially if they need me.

"Please come in Jenelle, you are considerably late after your ordeal toady. I was hoping it wouldn't take so long" Came a crackly, older, female voice from the other side of the door.

I slowly opened the door, feeling a little like I was outside my body watching myself. This woman had known I was there without me making a sound. She knew I had an ordeal today, and she knew it was me.

"Hello, I am finishing up a few things then I will explain everything to you. Please sit down at the table."

She bustled around her strange house. It was filled with odd bits in jars and bags. There were some things that could not be seen. There were dark bags that would wiggle occasionally and there were smells coming from all over. The most dominant was from a large cauldron on the fire.

"What are you making?" I asked tentatively.

"Stew for Kalian. I am going to deliver it with the medication for the burns and sores in his eyes. Jarita punctured them when they were protecting you. Her attack left holes in his layer of fire protection." she answered.

She moved around the cabin for a while. She knew where everything was. She never bumped into anything. As I watched her I noticed some strange things about her appearance. Though she sounded and had to have been an older woman she looked extremely young. There was a bandage around her eyes that was thin in both width and thickness. I could see the outlines of her eyes though them. The bandage only covered form right under her eyebrow to just above her cheek bone. She was short and thick but soft somehow. Her hair was dirty blonde with streaks of red through it and it was cropped close to her head. It looked like she might have tried to cut it herself.

"Alright, that should be ready by the time I get ready to head for the cavern." she said. Then she turned to me "What have you been told so far?" she asked.

"Only bits and pieces. I was told about you, of course, and how the fact that you can't see made it so you can see glimpses of the future. I was told my decisions could change the future you saw. I was told I am going to have a team to help me, but nobody told me what they are going to help me do. Ummm . . . . I think that's it, except for the fact that you have been seeing pieces of this future over a long period of time." I answered.

"Would you like me to start from the beginning? Or do you just want me to tell you what's missing and let you piece it together?" she asked.

"Start from the beginning, so I don't miss anything please."

She walked over to me and sat across the table from the chair I was in. "I started seeing glimpses of this impending future before you were born. About twenty years ago I saw a glimpse of a young figure helping the garden achieve full freedom from worry. These visions were blurry, because if your mother had taken a course that did not result in your birth it would not have been possible. After you were born the visions started to become more concrete. I tried to help as much as possible to aid the people to get to where they needed to go. After much time the visions still become more and more concrete. I felt this might be what is to come. I started using some of my more desperate measures."

"Desperate measures?" I couldn't stop myself from asking.

"Some of the tools I use that can help piece together my visions are not always good magic. But sometimes you need to use dark magic to make good things happen. I only use them when I am desperate for answers to my visions, and this was important enough to need them." she explained.

"I see, so you used dark magic to be able to see the foretelling?" I asked with a distrustful tone. I am not sure I liked the dark magic side of this.

"Yes, and it helped me find some of the more important details of the foretelling." She answered tersely, hearing my judgment in my tone.

"Which were?" I asked trying to keep the judgment out of my tone, and not entirely succeeding.

"After everything was decided, more or less a few years ago, the foretelling I had was this. After the child had reached eighteen years of life the opposing side would fight for domination. They would start with the garden then move to the world. The only weapon we would have to defeat them is this child, an ultimate cross breed. She will be victorious and all those who oppose her will fall. She will have an elite team to train and protect her through her conquest. This team will be made up of seven members of the garden. The nurturer will help her in a motherly way, as she does to all the other creatures in the garden. This would be Arhea. The strength will come from the unknown father. This is Kynis. The guardian will be there to prevent harm from happening to her in any circumstance. As I am sure Baellon has already stated. An unexpected relationship will be there to protect her heart from falling. This is Kethael. Shunned from both sides of her heritage, the outcast will provide determination and courage. As you have met Zula. The friend will support her and give her someone to confide in. This is a fae named Emerenta. I do not know if you have met her yet. And the last is a bird of fire that will bring out the core power in the victor. That is Jarita. This team will aid the victor in training and give her the support she needs to win this battle. But the most important thing is you are supposed to bring together the garden to get them to fight as one. Unity is going to be your greatest shield."

"I was told there was one more choice that could make all of this fail. What is it?" I asked

"The only choice left. Cant you see it?"

"No, I don't see that there really is a choice. I have a team, I unite the garden, and I win a battle. Where's the choice?"

"Everyone has a choice in every action. The plain choice that you fail to see here is that you don't."

"Don't what?" I was getting confused by this conversation, and trying really hard not to get irritated at that fact.

"Don't do anything. Let the opposing side of the island conquer us all. If you sit back and don't do anything, the future crumbles and shifts to a much darker place. I got a glimpse of it a few days ago. I suppose you were deciding whether or not you wanted to leave the garden. If you had left we would have lost before the battle began." this answer left me dumfounded.

"So my choices are fight and win with the team provided or don't fight and lose not only my freedom but everyone else's?"

"Yes, those are the choices at hand now you must choose."

"Those aren't really choices. I mean I guess they are but who would choose to lose when they know they would win if they fought?"

"Fear and weakness are almost as powerful as courage and strength child." she answered.

"Well, I am not scared or weak so I guess let the training begin."

"That, my dear, is wonderful news."

I had greeted Zula and Baellon outside after my discussion with the seer, and they were both thrilled that I had decided to accept the task at hand. Zula made plans to teach me physical combat, and wondered what Jarita could do for me. They both escorted me back to where the outcast part of the forest ends. Zula told me to come see her as soon as I was ready, and then left me with Baellon. We walked back towards my house. He had me follow him to the point where he would be staying in the woods. He told me to find him if I needed anything. I walked home alone and have been sitting here ever since.

I keep trying to come to terms with what I have agreed to. I am going into battle with creatures I don't know about yet. But if the seer is right, and I haven't heard her be wrong yet, I am going to win. I am going to have my team to help me too.

My team does seem to be reassuring, mostly. Emerenta being part of my team explains why she was so willing to give me information the day of the celebration. She must have known. The one that really seems to be nagging at the back of my brain is Kethael. The seer said something about my heart. This with Kethael's comment the other night was a little hard to deal with. If I am going into battle how could any kind of relationship like that be helpful? Wouldn't it be more of a distraction?

As I was sitting there thinking about Kethael there was a knock on my door. I went to answer it and, of course, it was him.

"How are you tonight, Jenelle?" Kethael asked.

"Okay, how about you?"

"I am well. I actually came to deliver a message. Arhea said to meet her at the willow the same time for your lessons, and to tell you she has the answers you requested."

"Okay. Thanks."

"Are you sure you are well?" he asked, taking in my tone of voice which sounded kind of dead, and the expression on my face.

"I went to see the seer today. I found out everything I need to know. I am just trying to make sure I understand everything.

I was sort of lost in thought when you arrived." I answered as honestly as I could, leaving out the fretting about him. I didn't think that would be productive.

"I see, would you like to go for a walk and talk about it? I am sure you have had a great deal to take in."

"Actually, I have had more than a great deal and I do not want to walk anymore. I had a run in with Kalian, which almost ended badly. I really just want to take a shower and go to sleep. I'm sorry. Maybe we can make plans to do this on a day where I am not so tired. Do you want to come back tomorrow and try again?" I felt bad for turning him down; even if I wasn't sure I wanted a relationship with him I did still want him as a friend.

"I understand, and am terribly sorry to hear about meeting Kalian. How did you manage to cross his path?"

"I have an entire team of people and wanted to meet them all and two of the members in the team were in the cavern. Jarita was keeping watch, and Zula had a plan but it ended in Zula flying me out while Baellon and Jarita held Kalian back. The seer was making him stew and medicine when I finally reached her house." I explained.

"Quite a day indeed. I will leave you to your sleep preparations and will come back tomorrow as you have requested. Sleep well." then he turned and left.

He didn't seem to be upset and that was a good thing I really didn't want to hurt his feelings.

I took a very long shower. It took a while to get the smell of the cavern out of my hair, plus I was extremely dirty form walking around all day. After I was finally clean I went to my room and got ready for bed.

When I was finally lying in bed I realized I could do this. I have always been a fighter. I fought my way through life since my mother died. I had to fight David, the people in the neighborhood, and even myself sometimes to make it through my life alive and in one piece.

With that reassurance I fell asleep.

CHAPTER 14
HERITAGE

I woke up early. I felt pretty good about the foretelling but was a little nervous about today. Kethael said that Arhea had got me the answers I requested. That meant that today I would find out exactly what I am made up of. This will be good and a little odd. I will figure out what I am exactly which I need to figure out what I can do, preferably before I go into this battle. It will be odd because up until about a week ago I thought I was just human, granted I didn't know there was another option.

After I got up and ready I headed towards the willow tree. Best to get the answers first and get it over with so I can get to my lessons. As I was walking towards the willow tree I was startled to hear someone following me. Last time I walked this way it was clear and uneventful. I was starting to get paranoid when I heard him.

"Good morning Jenelle" Baellon thought.

"You scared me" I answered with a laugh. "I forgot you were supposed to be my guardian. When you said you would follow me anywhere I didn't realize you meant you would follow me everywhere I went."

"I apologize but I fail to see the difference. I will follow you unless you specifically ask me not to, and even then it is against my better judgment for you to do this."

"Well, this morning it doesn't really matter. I am just going to the willow tree to see Arhea. You can come with me if it makes you feel better."

"Thank you"

Baellon stayed hidden close in the trees when we were almost to the willow tree. In his defense he was trying to be unobtrusive. I walked the rest of the short distance to the tree alone. Arhea was waiting for me outside the tree today with a small book in her hands.

"Good morning, Jenelle. How was your weekend? I am glad you got my message. I was going to have one of the girls come find you if you did not show up." Arhea seemed nervous. It made me anxious too.

"Let's just get the answers out of the way so we can get to whatever else there needs to be done today." I said trying not to be rude. My nerves helped a little in that department. It's hard to sound rude when your voice quivers and seems to have no volume.

She seemed a little apprehensive. I wonder if it was due to my response last time we met here. It seemed like she was trying to decide how to tell me. "I spent some time over the weekend collecting information form as many reliable sources and of course my own personal log of marriages and births. In this book are the answers you asked for. I traced back to the first cross breed in your family line. It is a little extensive. And like I said before it would be easier for me to tell you what you are not crossed with."

"Well, I am still learning most of the creatures so please tell me both, what I am and am not crossed with."

"As you wish," she opened her book "You are not crossed with centaur, earth elemental, elf, Pegasus or pixie. As a fae you were born with fairy magic, so that is a given, but you also are part air, fire and water elemental, mermaid, nymph, satyr, witch, dragon, phoenix, unicorn, and sphinx. How a wizard managed sphinx is beyond me but it happened."

I tried to catalog everything she said. It wasn't so bad. I had met almost all the creatures she said and they seemed mostly nice to me, except Kalian but I did have Baellon. "Can I have that book?" I asked, surprising even myself with my calm.

"Of course, I copied it for you, after all." She answered, watching me skeptically.

"So I need to figure which powers I have so I can use them right?" I asked "How do I do that?"

"Well first we need to access them. You have lived too much of your life ignoring them and being tarnished by the outside world. Your time here has helped you tremendously but we still need you to feel your powers before we can try to use them."

We spent the first part of the day with me accessing my powers. Fortunately I guess I had accessed some while I worked at the nursery because Arhea had said that it wasn't as hard as she thought it was going to be. When Arhea had felt I had unlocked the full potential for my powers we sat down to eat lunch. My power was an odd feeling. I felt like I was on some strange energy rush and most of my body tingled with the power.

When we had finished eating Arhea said "Now comes the difficult part to our lessons." She then looked at me as though she was trying to convey the importance of her words. "You will work with all your energy to utilize your powers. We must see what you can do so we will be trying everything and anything we can think of."

"How do I utilize my powers?" I asked.

"Channel them. You feel your power through your body do you not?"

"Yes, I think that's what it is at least."

"Focus on that feeling. Use the majority of your concentration and move the power from you body to your hands." She explained "Now let's go start."

She led me out into the forest to a small section around the back side. In front of where she stopped there were several small plants that looked like they had only recently been planted.

"We are going to start simple, with the fae magic. I want you to make this grow." She instructed pointing at one small bush.

"Okay . . . . ?" I knelt down next to the ground, nerves seeping through my body. What if I failed? How would they perceive me then? Would they think they made a mistake? Would they make me leave the garden? Arhea must have sensed my growing nerves, or seen them on my face.

"You are losing focus; do not worry about anything now. Focus on your energy and the bush only!" she commanded with a firm note in her voice.

I listened as well as I could. I pushed my worries to the back of my head. I would deal with them later if need be. I focused on the sensation moving through my body. I closed my eyes and envisioned the sensation as a tangible light. It shimmered behind my lids. I placed my hands heel to heel, with my fingers held straight side by side pointing opposite directions. Cupping them slightly around the bush I moved my light to my palms where it formed into a ball. Holding my ball of energy I pushed with all my might. I pushed the energy form myself to the bush with the only other thought being to make the bush grow. I heard Arhea gasp. I was afraid to open my eyes. I allowed small slits to form in my eyelids to see the source of Arhea's gasp. In front of me, where the small bush was, there was a fantastic, beautiful bush in its place. It was full and easily four feet tall covered in beautiful purple flowers.

"Well done Jenelle." She said with a tone that sounded like a mother who just found out her daughter was placed on honor roll.

We spent the next hour or so working on my fae power. It was amazing to see the wonderful things I could do. After I grew the first flower bush I enhanced three more. I enhanced the entire area Arhea had set for me. Then we moved to smaller targets. I planted several flower seeds, utilizing my power with each one, and then made them grow as soon as they were planted.

She wanted me to try to channel my powers without my hands. I was given more seeds and I was to enhance the seeds with my powers. After I planted them I was to make them grow only with my mind. This was much more difficult. It took me more then twice the amount of time to grow the seeds this way then with my hands.

We spent a fair amount of time after that working on mending plants. Arhea broke a small branch, wincing as she did this and apologizing to the tree. She told me to heal it and put it back together. This I was actually really good at. It only took me a second and I barely had to think about it.

"I think we have discovered that your fae powers are fully intact. The only other power I can help you with is your nymph power. Nymphs and fae are almost exactly alike with a few subtle differences. Nymphs are better at persuasion and attraction; it is part of how we survived as a race before the garden. So my advice to you is to utilize your powers when you need to be overtly persuasive. I wouldn't assume you need assistance in attraction since my sources tell me you have already attracted the attention from our friend Kethael." She smiled a very sly smile. I wasn't sure why but this made me feel the urge to blush and avert my eyes.

"Kethael and I are just friends. And what sources do you have?" I was trying to think of anyone who could have seen me.

"My sources are the trees and all other wild life in the garden." With this statement, a look of realization came across her face. "Oh my, we forgot to cover plant communication. I hear you do very well with animals so this should be easy."

We went back to work on the plants. It was harder to hear the plants than it was to hear the animals. Eventually though I got it. I found some very interesting things about plant life while we were at it. The flowers are arrogant. There thoughts consisted of vanity mostly and thinking they were all more beautiful then the next. The bushes were content. They reminded me of fat and happy cats that lay in the sunlight. Their only complaint is that the trees block them too much. The trees varied based on size and type. Some were dim witted. They seemed like airheads as they contemplated which direction to sway with the breeze. Some were tough, the oaks mostly. Their thoughts were as hard as their mass as they dared anyone to try and push them over. The willow however was an entirely different scenario. I understood why Arhea lived there. The willow was old, and she was wise. She knew that the others would fulfill whatever purpose they had even with their mismatched thoughts. She understood more then just the plant life. She also spoke with the wind and the animals. It was like talking to a grandparent that had lived through the changing times and was telling it from her point of view.

After this we were done with the powers Arhea could help me with. She seemed very pleased with me about what I had accomplished.

"I think we will end for the day." She had said after I sat at the base of the willow listening for over twenty minutes.

"Okay, thank you very much for your help. What will I be doing next, and who will help me?"

"I think you and I will continue practicing you powers here. We may move to healing more, especially animals but we must find an animal for you to use. I do not see how I would be able to provide one for you so we must wait on that. In the meantime we will continue your other studies. I will find you instructors to train you in your other areas of heritage and we will go form there." She answered.

"Sounds like a plan to me." We said our goodbyes and I left.

I walked with Baellon back home. Halfway home I remembered I had a walk with Kethael tonight. "Baellon, I have plans tonight, and not that I am ungrateful for your protection I will not be in any danger with this company. He is another one of my "elite team". I sort of don't want anyone else there. Do you mind not following me?" I was hoping he would not take offense to me asking him to stay behind.

"As long as you stay with a member of your elite team I do not see how this would be a complication. Just call my name if you need help. As long as you don't stray too far and you call loud enough I should hear you." He answered.

I was just relieved he wasn't upset. Our paths parted slightly when we were almost home. He left with the reminder that all I needed to do was call him and he would come to my rescue if I needed him to, which I doubted I would.

I waited for a very short time until Kethael arrived at my house. I don't know why but I was anxious to see him. He was one of the few members of my team that seemed to want to spend time with me for more reasons then because the seer said so. We walked into the forest again and he was silent. I don't know why, but he seemed unsure of what to say or do.

"Are you alright?" I asked

"Why do you ask?" he answered my question with a question of his own without answering mine.

"Well you just seem more quiet then you were the last time we walked." I answered hoping my answer would be rewarded with his.

I was wrong it was answered with another question "What answers did Arhea get for you?"

"I wanted to know exactly what I was made of so I could try to find my powers. She gave me a book with the list of my family tree."

"May I ask what all happened yesterday? You only gave me a brief description."

"I went to go find the seer yesterday. Nobody would tell me what the foretelling was because they said I needed to hear it from her myself. The first one I crossed was Zula, who pointed her lovely arrow at me. After it was clear who I was and that I wasn't a danger to her, she showed me around that part of the forest. She told me a little bit more about my team. When she mentioned the names of members she knew of, that I had never met, we went to the cavern. It was on part of my tour anyway but I don't think she intended for us to go into the cavern. That was my idea. We met Jarita first. Fortunately, my lineage allows me to hear the thoughts of the creatures here that don't speak. After a short discussion with Jarita we went down to meet Baellon. We had another short talk with him, and he gave a little more information when Kalian realized we were there. I rode on Zula out of his cave and we flew out of the cavern. After that we went to the seer and I went in alone. I got the entire foretelling, and a description of my entire team and what they are supposed to provide for me, one of them I have not really talked to about the foretelling. I only met her once and that was when I was getting ready for the celebration."

"And who is that?" he asked.

"Emerenta."

"I see, and what are we supposed to provide for you?" he asked. He kept a polite tone, but I could hear something hidden in his tone. I am not sure what it was.

"Each of you have a different purpose, Arhea is supposed to provide motherly support, Zula is supposed to be for courage, Baellon for protection, and so on and so forth. It's different for each person." I didn't want to talk about what he was supposed to be for or Kynis. Both seemed to be uncomfortable topics.

But of course he would ask "What am I supposed to be for?"

"Ummmm," I didn't want to get into this conversation but I guess I had no choice. I felt myself start blushing and couldn't make myself look him in the eyes. I stared at the ground and finally admitted in a small voice, "You are supposed to be the unexpected relationship to protect my heart."

"I see." He said then he fell silent for a while. I still couldn't bring myself to look at him. "So . . ."he seemed to be looking for the right way to phrase his next question.

"So?" I asked not sure whether or not I wanted him to ask.

"You do not want a relationship with me?" he asked.

I blushed deeper. I still hadn't figured out what I wanted. I have never even thought about relationships. My entire life I have focused on survival and escape. "Its not that I don't . . . um . . . . I'm not sure." I answered honestly. I figured if he was going to push this conversation then I should tell him the truth and the entire truth at that. "Listen, my entire life I have had two main thoughts, survival and escape." I explained my thoughts "I have never considered having a relationship; I don't even know how to start in that area. I have never even had any real friends. I mean I talked to my boss at work and a few teachers when I was in school but that's it since I was a little kid. And right now my focus should be on this foretelling and the coming battle." I tried to get it all out before my throat closed up again or I started crying. This entire situation was frustrating. I was worried about the battle and at the same time about hurting his feelings. I did like him but I haven't decided how I like him and it wasn't fair for him to push this conversation.

"But the seer says that our relationship is to help you win the battle, correct?" he asked.

This stopped me short. All my frustration and worry seemed to be wiped form my brain. It wasn't out of relief but of shock. "I . . . um . . . . but . . . um . . . . she didn't really . . . . well . . . ." I didn't know what else to say. I guess she did sort of say that in a round about way. She said my team was to help me win and she said what they were for so I guess putting them together that is what she had said.

"Listen Jenelle, I am not going to try to make things difficult, nor am I going to try and force a relationship on you." He said with a small laugh. "You look like you are waiting for some sort of attack. You are overly defensive and need to relax. Trust the seer. She knows what is going to happen and I am sure she has an understanding of the complications of things. I highly doubt she expected you to hear that and have you and I elope, so please relax. We can continue how we have been, for you say you have not had any real friends. Maybe that is the relationship she speaks of. Relationships come in many different ways." He continued to explain in a soothing voice.

"I don't think that's the kind of relationship she was talking about. Emerenta is supposed to be the friend for me to confide in." I answered in a weary voice. I really didn't want to say we should be together but I am almost positive that's what the seer meant. And his comment on eloping had me on edge.

"Well, regardless of what she may or may not have meant, let us just continue how we have been. Even if that's where we are supposed to lead, it does not necessarily mean that is where we must start." He said. I finally was able to make myself look up at him. He was smiling, and I couldn't help return it. I was relieved that he was not expecting anything.

After our conversation he walked me back home. I was glad that we had a chance to talk but was also relieved it was over. I was completely exhausted. I was mentally and physically drained from my training this morning and my conversation with Kethael was emotionally debilitating. I was ready for some serious sleep.

CHAPTER 15

TRAINING

Over the next few weeks I trained harder than I would have thought possible. I spent hours every morning with Arhea. We worked relentlessly on growing, healing, and communicating with plants. It was exhausting and monotonous. After a couple of days I had it down but she insisted on practicing so I wouldn't lose any of it. We also did some more history and I learned about all the different plants in the garden. After a while I started training with Kynis too. I was pretty good at witch work but there was more to learn here. I was constantly learning new ways of healing and other potions. It was a good thing that I was given new books to put all this into or I would not be able to get much use out of it. So far these were the only two I had practiced with.

I walked with Beallon, who accompanied me to my training everyday, to the willow tree. We walked in silence toady. We finally reached the tree and I was very surprised to see that Arhea was not alone. There were several people standing there with her.

"Good morning." I said hesitantly as I approached the group of people.

"I have realized that not only have you mastered your plant work but no longer wish to continue with solely these practices. In addition I have no more history to teach you. From this moment on we will be splitting your training with several teachers." Arhea had explained without waiting for the question. "Once a week you will meet here with me to assure that you still understand plant communication and have no questions on history or origins, Emerenta will be accompanying you for this. From here Emerenta will walk you to Kynis for your potion work. The following day you will spend time on your water abilities. Araxia is one of the mermaids who reside in the rivers through out the garden and she will be helping you as well as the water elemental Dwynwen. The next day will be to you air and fire elemental properties. Airella and Nimiat will cover those for you. The day after you will work with Baellon, Eilsy, and Jarita to cover any animal like powers you may possess. On the final day of the week you will meet with Zula. Although we hope it will not come to this, Zula feels you need combat skills and I cannot argue with her logic. Her centaur nature will be able to help you in that area since I have failed to get the centaurs to help much in this matter. Eiriden here" she gestured to the satyr at her side "will be accompanying you to these training sessions for he will be learning, to in turn train the other satyrs as a precaution."

"So, five days a week then?" I summed up the explanation.

"Yes, your weekend will be for you to do as you like." Arhea confirmed.

"Okay so today will be with who?" I asked. Trying to remember what order I was supposed to go in.

"Ariella and Nimiat. You will work on air and fire today." Arhea said indicating the two elementals off to the side. They were both elementals, Ariella was one of those whose frame shifted like parts of her were blowing in the breeze and Nimiat was flickering like a flame. He seemed to be upset about this arrangement. I wondered if he really wanted to be there.

"I will work with you first, if you don't mind" Ariella said. Her voice was whispy and sounded as though it was brought by the light breeze around us.

"That's fine." I replied. Even though I used my normal voice it sounded like shouting compared to hers.

Then Nimiat said "After you're done playing with the wind I will work with you, but not here, so you will have to meet me towards the cavern. If you don't know how to get there have Baellon show you." His voice was the exact opposite to Ariella's. It was deep and rough. He sounded as angry as he looked. After his instructions he turned on his heel and headed towards the direction of the cavern.

"We will work just on the other side of these trees. There is a small meadow that I think will prove most useful to help us try to work today." Ariella instructed. As she said this the others turned and left as well. Arhea smiled at me and turned to go back inside the willow tree. I followed Ariella into the trees and, as she said, we came into a small but beautiful meadow. It had grass that rose to about my knee cap.

The sole purpose of this training was for me to try and conjure the wind. It was just as easy as getting the plants to grow or talking to animals. I just had to close my eyes and ask the wind to come. We worked with getting it to come and go and even swirl around me like a vortex. Areilla said this would prove to be a useful weapon if I could increase force and send around another person. She didn't want to try though because she said it would cause unnecessary harm to another.

After that I met Baellon and we went to the cavern. This lesson, again, was easy. Nimiat was pleased with how easy I could conjure fire and at one point in time I was able to get it to come from my finger tips. It was just a flicker and then it went out, but it was there for a second. Nimiat said this was due to the mixture of fire creatures in my blood. We burned for a while and when it was almost dusk he said we were finished. We would work on more intricate flames the next week.

The following day was the same. There really wasn't much I could do since the animal powers only increases what my other powers needed Fire and healing. Baellon tested whether or not I could be burned so he set a fire and instructed me to carefully set my hand in the flame. I felt a small tickle as the flames brushed my skin but that was it. My defenses were the same as his and Jarita's.

Friday proved to be the most difficult yet. I could not fight or shoot at all. I apparently can't even hold a bow right. After several hours of utilizing the apparent grace I got from other places in my body, we decided it was going to take a lot more work.

Saturday morning I was awaken by a light knocking on the door. I got up to answer it and was surprised to see Emerenta.

"Good morning. I thought we should start spending some more time together. I am sure you heard what my part in this is and if we are going to be friends we should get to know each other better." She said and smiled. She stood there for a minute until my half asleep brain caught up.

"Oh I'm sorry, please come in."

We spent most of the day together and as I thought from the beginning, she was easy to be friends with. We shared stories, though hers took more time since she had much more of a life than I had before I came to the island. I did decide to divulge that technically she was my aunt. She thought that bit of information was intriguing. This was the one topic I was able to tell a decent length story. I even showed her the letters and my mother's journal. When she finally left some time after lunch I felt like I had known her my entire life.

That night when the sun started to set Kethael came to my house too. This time we just sat outside in the front yard and talked. I asked if he knew where to go for furniture for outside and he said he did. He said I could have Emerenta take me to go see the elf that could do it best. He couldn't because they weren't on very good terms.

Sunday was much the same. Emerenta took me to get the outdoor furniture and I also put in an order for a few other things like picture frames, another bookshelf, some more furniture for the living room and kitchen, and some new cupboards for my bathroom. We went to another person who did a full order of kitchen ware. Emerenta and I did an entire day of shopping. We made an order for clothes that she thought I would like and some I was scared to see when I got them. We made a large order for food since I hadn't done it since I had come to the garden and I was running out. She also insisted on a full line of beauty products to fill my bathroom cabinets. We talked and shared the entire way. It got a little awkward when she asked about Kethael, who she heard from someone was supposed to be my lover. I blushed and stammered through out the explanation and she seemed like she didn't like my response. Her look was sour as she sad "Kethael is a little off but he is extremely good looking. You could do worse you know." After which I had to assure her that it had nothing to do with his demeanor or looks that had me on edge.

Everyone who was responsible for making the furniture and other items seemed very willing to give me there service. Whether it was because they knew my mother or because they knew about the foretelling, I don't know.

Sunday night Kethael met me at my doorstep and we went for a small walk. I could hear Baellon in the trees but he remained out of sight and Kethael didn't mention hearing him. We talked about things that were not important. I told him what I did and what I got that day.

The following week was much the same as the last. The main differences were that my lessons changed slightly and I grew closer to Emerenta. The weekend was also much the same. I seemed to have my weekend days split into two and I spent my days with Emerenta and my evenings with Kethael. Week three for my new training regime seemed a little monotonous and mundane. It started to turn into nothing but review. I was able to master each new challenge before the day was over. After we made it back to Wednesday my lessons all seemed conquered. There wasn't much I couldn't do. After my lessons I went to talk to Arhea.

"Sorry to bother you but I wanted to talk to you about my lessons." I said when I met her outside.

"What about your lessons?" she asked.

"I don't know if I want to train every day for one thing. I am having no difficulties with anything that has to do with my abilities. The only thing I feel I still need to work on is my battle training. So, I was wondering if I could make my own schedule?" I explained.

"I don't see why that would be a problem. As long as your ideas don't interfere with the plans of those you need help from."

"Well I wanted to try and only train with my abilities once a week at most and then spend the rest of my time learning battle skills."

"What do you mean by at most?" she asked to clarify.

"Well I really don't see what I need much from training with everyone. I think I don't need my fire elemental teacher. I learn all of what he teaches me and more with Baellon and Jarita. And Eilsy is great but I really don't need her training because my unicorn powers are not really something I can train with. But mostly I don't think my time is doing more than exhausting me and I don't think that I should be exhausted if I am supposed to go into battle."

"So how would you like to train your abilities and how often?" again she asked to clarify.

"I would like to practice on my own but be able to get in contact with the people I need help from. The only instructor I want to practice with on a regular basis is Zula."

"Which instructors do you want to be able to contact or do you want access to all of them?" she asked.

"I would like to access all of them please"

"Okay I will get you any and all information. I will let your instructors know that you will not be joining them you can make arrangements with Zula about your training sessions. Go see her tomorrow but I suggest that you wait until the afternoon."

"Why wait until the afternoon?" I asked.

"Zula partakes in some activities during the morning that she prefers to do alone. If you interrupt her it may decrease your chances of further help or guidance."

"Okay, I think. Thank you."

I turned around to leave. I walked home and Baellon met up with me.

"How long do you think until you are ready for battle?" he asked.

"I guess I don't know. I don't think I will ever be ready for it but I think I will feel a little better after my battle skills are a little more defined. My powers are developing nicely though"

He didn't have much to say after that. When I got home all of my orders from Sunday were sitting outside of my house along with Emerenta who was waiting for me.

"I helped deliver your things and thought I would wait for you to see if you wanted help setting up or decorating or just wanted some company?" she babbled very quickly. Part of me wondered if she only wanted to spend so much time with me because the seer said we would be friends, but I can't deny that from the moment I met Emerenta I felt we could be friends.

"Thank you, I would like some company and it might be helpful to have an extra pair of hands to move some of the furniture." I said with a smile. She beamed back and seemed genuinely pleased for me to have accepted her offer.

We moved in all of the furniture, rearranged the existing furniture, set up the outside furniture, went through the clothes, put all of my new beauty products into the bathroom, and then sat around for a while going through pictures to put in frames. I was happy that the house seemed to gradually feel more like mine as the time passed. I was happy to be in my mother's old house and it would always be a link to her but I didn't like feeling like I was staying in someone else's house.

The next day I went to go see Zula. I waited until the afternoon as Arhea had instructed and met her close the edge of the woods.

"Hello Jenelle, what can I do for you? It is not time for your training." She had said as soon as she saw me.

"I am sorry to bother you; I actually wanted to talk to you about my training sessions."

"Alright, you talk I will listen but please let us get to the point I have a few things I need to do still this day." She answered.

"I am really sorry for keeping you" I started to say but she gave me an exasperated look that made me jump to the point. "I have mastered all of my other lessons as much as I can be trained except my battle skills. I was wondering if we could practice and train more throughout the week. I already talked to Arhea and she said that I needed to talk to you about it." I said as quickly as I could without stammering or slurring my words.

"I see, well I will see what I can do for you, but I do have other obligations to tend to."

"Do you mind if I ask you a couple of personal questions?" I asked timidly.

"You may ask but I will not guarantee an answer." She replied.

"Why couldn't I come in the morning? Arhea warned me not to. And what other obligations do you have? I thought you wouldn't have anything since you live in this part of the forest."

She seemed slightly ashamed and also a little angry. "For your information, just because one lives in this part of the woods does not mean they do not prove to be useful. I run surveillance for Arhea. As for what I do in the morning, well that is my business. Arhea only knows vaguely what I do and out of respect for me she does not ask questions and she also assists me in keeping people out of my way." She seemed very angry at me. I felt bad for asking but I guess it's in my nature to question everything. I still sometimes question everything about this place.

"I'm sorry for asking. I will not interfere or question your mornings again. But can I help with your surveillance?" I was hoping to redirect the conversation back to my training. It seemed to work a little. She still seemed irritated but not as angry as before.

"I am not sure whether or not that is a good idea." She answered vaguely.

"I promise I will do what you ask and I won't get in the way. Please I really want to feel more comfortable with my battle skills. I don't want to lose this because I am not prepared, I need your help." I pleaded.

"It is not that I feel you will be in my way. You are precious to this victory, without you we will fail. I feel there is more to the future than the seer is telling us but I am sure she has her reasons and we will be enlightened in due time. I rarely encounter a problem when I am patrolling the border but I am not sure I should risk it with you." She explained.

"Maybe we could bring Baellon and Kethael. It would help to have extra hands and eyes plus maybe I could get a little more practice and have you to help fine tune my technique?" I suggested.

She didn't look too happy about this situation but she seemed torn on the matter. "Fine" she conceded "if you can get them to agree to come along and you all agree to do as I say, then I will agree to help as much as possible. Meet me here at the same time tomorrow with both of them." She agreed.

That night I was able to get both of them to agree. Neither of them seemed too happy to be under Zula's orders but they only grumbled about it, not openly protested.

CHAPTER 16

WARNING

The morning came faster than I would have thought. I was both very nervous and excited about the days training. It made my sleep restless. After I finally dragged myself out of bed, I started to get ready. Some of the outfits I picked out when I was shopping with Emerenta were more suited for my liking and also my needs. I picked outfits that were designed for excess movement, with a few alterations. After finding out about what magic could do to clothes I placed a few special orders designed for my battle. I selected a beige shirt that was not exactly loose but it wasn't tight either to allow my arms to move freely. To pair with this, as suggested by the witch helping me, I also got a leather corset. It laced up the front with black draw strings which complimented the dark brown leather. This allowed my arms to stay free but for the loose material around my torso to be pulled tightly in the right spots. The pants were black and although they were tight they were made of a breathable and flexible material. It was almost impossible to tear this material, with the exception of a metal blade. The pants stopped just below my knees. The boots I selected for this outfit both served as extra protection as well as durability. The leather was supple and bent freely. They rose to my mid thigh to protect from blade attacks on my tendons and arteries through most of my legs. The leather matched the corset. And the final piece of the outfit was not only the most useful but also the only one that wasn't seen. It was more of a body sheath. It was worn beneath my clothes and was a flesh colored material. It came in four pieces (the witch seemed to insist on the outfit to be flattering as well as useful, even though this wasn't a concern of mine). The bottom piece solidly covered me from my waist down, even securing my feet. The second piece covered from my waist up to just above my breast, covering my heart without hindering any cleavage allotted from the corset and the thin strip missing from the shirt that laced loosely down the front of my chest. The last two pieces were arm cuffs. They reached from my under arms to my wrists. The most fascinating trait of my body sheath was not the fact that it covered most of my body, or the fact that it didn't hinder my ability to move or appear flashy; it was the fact that whatever this material was made out of made my skin almost impossible to get to. The witch displayed this by thrusting a pair of shears at it with all of her force, and not even a split appeared in the material.

After I was dressed, cleaned up, and had breakfast I headed outside. It was almost time to head out and meet Zula. Baellon was waiting for me in plain view and Kethael was actually sitting in my outdoor furniture. Baellon stepped forward and Kethael stood up, signaling they were ready to go without saying a word. We walked in silence to the edge of the outcast part of the forest. Zula seemed both surprised and irritated that we were there. I don't think she thought the other two would agree to the terms. Regardless she had made a deal and Zula wasn't the type to go back on her word.

"Don't forget that you must do as I say. We are not to initiate or engage in unnecessary combat. Our main goal is to keep our eyes open for anyone crossing the border, but as we go we will practice in different fighting maneuvers. I have gathered new weapons for you Jenelle. I had them crafted specifically for you and they should fit well. I also had a few accessories for your ensemble crafted for you to help you carry your weapons" Zula explained.

The weapons and accessories were wonderful. I had a belt/ harness that wrapped around my waits and looped up over one shoulder. The belt part had a sheath that was a perfect fit for a beautifully crafted sword. The sword was not too long and was also extremely light weight. The hilt curved down just enough to help secure my hands in place. There were also pockets and smaller sheaths for me to place other tools I thought would be helpful. The harness part had two small loops in it. One was for a staff that was also beautifully crafted. It looked like a walking stick from a distance but up close you could see the engravings on the sides. It looked like inscriptions. The other loop held a bow. I also had a sheath of intricate arrows. The way they all fit, they were both functional and only added to the beauty of the outfit. I was both beautiful and lethal.

"We must be going" Zula said as soon as I was fitted with my new apparel.

We headed to the border in silence. When we reached the border of the garden Zula turned on us, she looked stern but not hostile.

"So how would you prefer us to work?" Kethael asked with a note of petulance in his voice.

"I would like Jenelle to practice with her sword and staff for now. You two can help her with partnering and techniques, I will advise as I see fit." She answered undisturbed by his tone.

"You want me to attack them?" I asked shocked at her comment on partnering.

"Well not exactly, I want them to attack you and you to defend yourself." She answered seeming as if nothing was out of the ordinary.

"What if I hurt one of them or the other way around? Are you sure this is the best way to approach this?" I could hear a note if hysteria in my voice.

"It is the only way to proceed Jenelle" she answered and it was comforting to hear that she sounded concerned and sincere at the same time.

"Do not worry Jenelle, we will be fine and I am sure under these circumstances you will prevail and we would not be able to harm you even if we wanted to." Kethael tried to soothe me.

"How do you know you will be fine? If I am going to prevail that means I will hurt you."

"*Well then I guess it's a good thing that you have already mastered your healing then?*" Baellon answered sarcastically.

"That is not funny, Baellon!" I snapped. He made a strange sound that sounded like a cross between a bark and choking, which I assumed was laughing since it was in unison with the laughing in his head.

"What did we miss?" Kethael asked.

"He said it was good I mastered my healing abilities." I explained. Kethael started laughing. I did not find this in any way amusing. I glared at him and realized that Zula was fighting to keep the smile off her face too.

"All of you are not amusing!" I said.

"Just do as you are told. That was part of the agreement in your training." Zula had said.

"Fine!"

As we walked we practiced starting with the staff. I wanted to practice with something that wasn't as threatening first until I got the hang of it. Baellon and Kethael did not hesitate on their attacks. For the first few rounds I was down quickly. At one point in time Baellon swooped down and caused a ruckus with his wings that distracted me long enough for Kethael to tackle me to the ground and disarm me. Every time I was close to losing or had lost Zula would bark out instructions like "watch your footing!", "Focus" or "keep your eyes open". Every time I would fumble with one of her previous instructions. She was starting to get annoyed and her instruction started sounding more like insults.

Finally I managed to save myself from an attack. Baellon had swooped over me and I ducked in just enough time to swing my staff out as Kethael approached. I caught him right at the ankles and knocked his legs out from underneath him.

"Very good Jenelle." Zula complimented. "I think I have had an idea on how to train you better in your fight." She added.

"How is that?" I asked skeptically.

"You shall see tomorrow. Today is coming close to an end and as night grows closer I need to focus on my surveillance. Meet the same time as tomorrow." She said.

Baellon, Kethael, and I walked back towards my house. Baellon veered off and went to his place in the woods close to my house but Kethael walked me to the door. "I know you will be fine. You just need to find the confidence in yourself." He said softly.

"How am I supposed to find confidence? I have never been in a fight." I asked.

"You have always been in a fight Jenelle. Once you see there is no difference in fighting to survive and fighting in battle you will see that you are a skilled fighter." He answered in the same soft voice . . . it was unnerving having him speak to me like it was his last breath he was using.

"Fighting to survive only meant that I kept my head down and my mouth shut. I didn't walk out into the middle of my neighborhood bearing weapons and challenging anyone! This is me going into a fight willingly, with the only hope being the seer saying I would win." I could hear panic creeping in my voice. I usually tried not to think about the battle too much. Even when I am practicing I only focus on the training not what I am training for. "Everyone is putting their hope in me that I can somehow save them all when I am not even sure what I am going to be fighting. All I know is that the woman on the other side of the island has unpleasant creatures, that she doesn't like normal humans, and that she and Arhea used to be friends." My body was full with a mixture of emotions. I was scared and angry at the same time. I was torn between my want to protect everyone at risk, wanting to scream at the top of my lungs, and the part that wanted to cower and hide. "What part of my life has everyone misunderstood? I am not good at fighting; I am good at running and hiding."

"Jenelle" Kethael said in a voice that sounded surprised and impressed at the same time.

"What now? Please don't say any more about how you think I can do this. I can't take it."

"Jenelle look." He said in a firm but still impressed voice. He was point at my hands as he told me to look so I followed instructions confused, and looked down at my hands.

I gasped. My hands seemed to be holding several things at once, and then I realized that the substances were coming from my hands. It was as if water and fire were being pulled into a vortex in my hands. Streams of crystal clear water and jets of a deep red flame were twisting on my hand as though they were forming a tornado. The misty substance between them looked like angry clouds fighting to force the water and fire to work together. As I looked around myself it seemed the battle was more than just my hands, my entire yard was being blown around as if the wind decided to attack this one particular spot. Stunned and not sure what made me do it I focused on the flame in my hand and cast it to the ground near me, it caught on the stone but still blazed on, not burning anything but itself. I then set the water to the flame, they seemed to continue their little dance for a while before the water finally overtook the flame and extinguished it, then spilled across the ground.

"When you realize what you are capable of, you will be able to do anything you set your mind to." He said in an awed voice, leaned down and kissed my cheek, then turned to leave.

I stood there dumbfounded for an immeasurable time. My brain was having a hard time distinguishing my thoughts. First was the shock at the fact that I had conjured water, fire, and wind in my hands. I could still feel the elements coursing though my body. I could even feel the fourth. I felt grounded even as the wind swept through me, the water flowed, and the heat of the flame burned. The heat was from two different locations. I could feel the heat from the flame of course, but then there was a heat I was sure had nothing to do with fire. It burned in my stomach, my chest and on my face, in the spot where Kethael kissed my cheek. It was not an unpleasant feeling entirely, except maybe in my stomach where it felt like the heat was beating against the sides of my stomach with severe strength. My brain tried to catch up to the rest of my body.

Slowly, I started to have thoughts link together. First was the thought of Kethael and the heat in my body. Maybe it was that, even without consciously deciding, we were indeed moving past our friendship into something more complicated. I decided I would not interfere. I will not stop it or encourage it but that's all I can do at this point. The next thought I had connected the feeling of the elements coursing through my body and my battle training. I might be able to combine the two. I stood there for a minute thinking about what I wanted to do. I would have to try some of it out tomorrow.

<hr />

The next day Baellon and Kethael met me outside of my door. We walked in silence to where we were supposed to meet Zula. It was a little awkward for me, especially after Kethael kissed me last night. I was also trying to figure out how best to use my new found power in battle.

Zula met us and we went directly to business. As we walked along the perimeter of the garden Baellon and Kethael started in on their attacks. I was still using my staff and this was good since I wanted to experiment with my new power I really didn't want any accidents. The first attack shocked both Baellon and Zula, but Kethael having witnessed last night, smirked at me. They both had charged at me from opposite sides. I lashed a line of blazing flames to block Kethael's path, and propelled water at Baellon. With this I was able to hold my ground without moving too much and block them both. Zula was very impressed. After a very short while she stopped us.

"The idea I had yesterday seems that it might even prove more useful with this new found power. I have set up an agility training course for you. If you use the combination of your fighting, power, and movements you will never be challenged." With this she showed me this interesting set up a little ways up that was made of mounds, tunnels, hoops and poles. I had to jump the mounds, roll through the tunnels, flip through hoops, and move in an alternating motion between the poles. It was a severe workout but as I was practicing I could see what Zula meant. I was fast and agile. I started throwing my own movements in this course. I would jump the mound practicing loading my bow in the process, when I rolled through the tunnels I would pull my staff as I righted myself. I threw wind, fire, and water at invisible targets as I twisted, flipped, and turned. I even was able to pull jagged rocks from the earth and use them as a shield.

All three of them had stopped to watch me practice. I was feeling my confidence build as I worked. Maybe I could do this. I was learning quickly and nothing could touch me if I didn't want it to.

But it couldn't be trusted to last.

A horrible screeching came from close to the border. Zula must have known what it was because she summoned a small nymph from a tree. She appeared out of the trunk and Zula gave her instructions. "I need you to bring me the team. Send word through the trees and get them all here now." She ordered. The nymph disappeared back into her tree and soon I could hear footsteps and wings. Arhea appeared out of a tree,

Kynis and Emerenta came running into the area and Jarita flew down her wings slightly blazing and her eyes tight with caution.

"We will move to the border as a unit. Jenelle in the center, Emerenta and Kethael bring up the rear, Baellon and Jarita take the sides, and me and Zula will take point. Do not break formation, no matter how we may be provoked. This is just a meeting; there will be no warning for battle. If they wanted to attack they would have." Arhea spoke calmly.

In formation we walked to the border. The sight at hand was enough to make me forget how well I was doing in training. There were two men like creatures; well they looked to have the body of men and the upper torso and head of a bull. The women perched up in the trees looked like they were part crow. They had long black winged arms, talon like toes, and beaks for faces. Taking point was a woman whose lower half of her body was the body of a large spider. Looking close at the patterns I recognized them at once. She was half black widow.

The spider woman stepped forward. She spoke in a raspy, hissing voice "Arhea, my lost friend, when will you understand that what I want is best. We could rejoin forces you understand that don't you?" she asked. Then she looked at me "This is you victor? Look at her! She is mere child with not very much magical potential in my opinion. I can't even see the magic in her skin. The seer said it would be an ultimate cross breed, not this." She stopped at the look of shock on all of our faces when she spoke of the seer. "Oh yes, I forgot to mention at our last meeting that I have too acquired a seer. Granted mine is not as humble as yours, as she uses older more practical means of prediction. She was not born with a sight like yours however. I would still love access to your seer and compare." She said with an evil grin.

"What do you want form this meeting Alicia?" Arhea asked getting to the point.

"To warn you that if you do not cease in trying to train this child to defeat me in a poor attempt, then I will be forced to obliterate your entire half of the island. You have one month's time to stop your actions and I suggest you get rid of the child." She answered maliciously.

"Why can you not see reason Alicia? All I want is peace. I understand your views on the outside world but why can you not just let them be and allow those who possess the gifts we admire to be welcomed and safe here with us?

"We will have peace Arhea. You will see when I purge the world of those who are of closed mind and are not worthy of our island. You will thank me one day, that is as long you head my warning and do not try to stop me. If you fail to follow through with my instructions then I will be forced to destroy you as well and you will not be here to appreciate what I am going to do." She answered.

"As you wish Alicia." Arhea said and then she turned to the rest of us. "This is the end of this meeting. Let's get back to the garden. Please all of you meet me at the willow tree." She waited for all of us to turn. We stayed in formation until we reached the original point where we had met up. Then Arhea left through a tree. The others spread more casually around me but did not leave. We walked in silence headed for the willow tree. All of us had the meeting and warning in our heads. For me however I was trying to decipher what Arhea meant when she told Alicia as she wished. Did that mean that she was going to give up and get rid of me? What was I going to do if she told me to leave?

CHAPTER 17

DECISION

When we reached the willow tree there was a table waiting for us. Emerenta, Kynis, Kethael, and I took seats close to Arhea and Baellon, Jarita, and Zula placed themselves around the empty space at the other end of the table. Arhea looked around at all of us with a grave look on her face.

"We all knew we were going to have to go into battle. Now we see that it is inevitable that we must fight to keep the world safe. If we give in, then all those in the outside world will be obliterated. We will be forced under Alicia's rule and this will mean leaving the life of peace we have behind. If we fight, we must fight until we are sure that there is nobody left from the other side to carry on Alicia's plan. That is a lot of life lost at our hands, but it is to save an even greater number of innocent lives." She paused, whether to collect her thoughts or give any of us the chance to say something I am not sure, but since she went uninterrupted she continued "What I need now is to know whether or not we are all still devoted to this?" she asked. At this point in time she directed her attention to Kynis who was sitting on her right side.

"I am devoted to protecting the life of the outside world as well as those in the garden." He answered formally.

Arhea then turned to Emerenta, "And you?" she asked.

"I will fight to protect the life we have created here and the life that remains ignorant in the outside world."

Baellon and Jarita both nodded in consent.

"It is not in my nature, nor in my desire, to turn away from this fight. I will fight and I will take as much life as necessary to protect life as a whole." Zula answered before Arhea could ask.

"Kethael, this must be a unanimous decision. If we are going to move forward your answer as well as Jenelle's will make the difference." She said to Kethael.

"I will follow Jenelle." He answered. I felt my face go red. "If she chooses to stay and fight then I will do all in my power to protect her but the same applies if she cannot or will not continue. I will follow her and protect her under any circumstance." He answered fully.

"Well Jenelle, then the final word rests with you." She said turning to me. All the others had their eyes on me as well. They were all waiting for my response. I could not think straight. Both options ended in lives lost and both risked my life but that was not my concern. Everyone in the garden faced death if I moved forward; if I do not fight then they face imprisonment but life. I could not decide which fate was worse.

"I need more time to think about it. Let me think about it tonight and I will let you know" I pleaded. I didn't want to make a fast decision and regret it later.

"Of course" Arhea answered. "I will call a meeting tomorrow, we will have your answer then and we will see where the garden as a whole stands. Those who will fight with us will be trained and those who cannot or will not fight will be protected."

As we rose from around the table I started walking in opposite direction of the village, my home, and the other side where those who want my death stay. Baellon, Zula, and

Kethael followed me. They did not try to stop me or even really catch up; they just trailed behind me watching silently.

I didn't know where I was going, or why really. My brain was confused, I am not sure what thoughts jumbled around or what was pushing me forward. It must have been hours before I remembered I was followed. I turned to find my entourage, to see what they were doing. When I turned I didn't see them, this confused me even more. I turned on the spot to see if I missed them. I guess they left me alone. I continued to walk for a while more until I realized the ground under my feet had changed. It wasn't grass or rock but sand. The sand was pearl white and shimmered in the rays of sun that broke through the trees. It was only a few more feet before I was blinded.

At first it's the brightness that blinds me. I have been sheltered by trees from the sun for so long now that it was hard to adjust. Then I understand that it is so bright because it is being reflected all around me. The sand and water, even the rocks glistening under the moisture are brighter. The smell of the ocean is unbelievable. I walked forward until the waves crashed over my toes. The water was surprisingly warm. I walked along the beach until I reached the rocks at the edge of the sea and ocean. I climbed up and found the perfect place. The rock was flat and jutted out just barely over the ocean. The waves crashing against it showered me with a spray. I sat and stared out at the ocean, the setting sun, the birds flying over head. I listened to the wind, the waves, and the sounds of life from a distance that I assumed to be the residents of the garden. Even though I was listening so hard I don't hear him come up.

"I told the others I would keep an eye on you so they could go home." Kethael said softly behind me. I jumped a little, and then turned to look at him.

He truly was gorgeous. With the sun and waves reflecting off of his skin he seems like he is shining too. "Do you just care about me because of the prophecy?" I asked before I could even think about what I was saying. I guess this was one of the things that were bothering me. Even if is menial.

He laughs a nervous laugh. "No." was all he answered and then looked to the rocks.

Well this answer wasn't enough for me. I was tired of having few things explained to me until it is too late, and even then most of the answers only raise more questions. "Then why? You barley know me" I asked to make him explain further.

"It is hard to explain. With my chosen isolation I have not been near anyone to be able to feel anything for so long it is hard to put into words the first strong feeling I have had."

"Try. Please."

He sat down beside me, staring out at the ocean as he started to speak slowly. "You seem to affect me in strange ways. When I am around you I feel happy, and nervous, and scared all at the same time. You make me want to protect you and let you shine. I feel like your loss would be my loss, your failure a failure of my own to help you succeed. At night when you are at home and probably asleep, I think of what it would be to hold you while you dream. When I am asleep I have dreamed about spending every waking moment with you from the time I have met you. You seem to have stamped your impression in my brain, it doesn't matter what I am doing or where I am, you are always either in the front of my mind or there as a hidden motive to help you or make you happy, and even sometimes my motive is to hope to make you love me." He blushes, looked at me sheepishly out of the corner of his eyes, and gives a bashful grin. "And I have given more than you asked; you seem to affect my brain in more ways than I thought."

I don't know if it was his speech, or the ocean, or the stress of the day. It could be the beauty of the sunset or his smile or the fact my heart was racing and my breath accelerated, but not of fear this time. This emotion was new to me. I lean in and kissed his unsuspecting mouth. He gasps in shock, but then slowly starts to kiss me back. It is the first real kiss I have ever had. I feel like a warm, tingling gel was sliding down my back, over my chests and arms. When it reached my toes I wrapped my arms around his neck. He placed his hands softly on my hips. But then he stopped. I looked at him confused; I didn't know what I was doing or why he pulled away. He gave me a quizzical look.

"Please do not misunderstand this next question as a complaint, for I have no complaint to give, but where did that come from?"

"I don't know" I answer, then was embarrassed when I realize I was breathless. The moment of senseless emotion had passed. I really don't understand why I kissed him or what I was feeling. It all made my brain more jumbled as I tried to think about it. I dropped my arms and stepped back.

"Why don't I walk you home? You need your rest before you go to the meeting and give them our vote in the morning."

Well there went any resemblance of a good mood. As I got up I realized what thought had been jumbling around in my head. It fell out of my mouth as if my standing up pushed it out. "Who am I?"

He looks at me confused. "Jenelle?" he answers as if it was a question. Hoping he understood my question and got the answer correct, I think.

"I know that. That's not what I meant. I know my name; I meant my personality, my sense of self. Since I came to the garden I have lost all of my core traits. Not that they were pleasant but they were who I had to be to survive. Who am I now that I have gone soft in the garden? All I have is my practice and fighting with finding out I never truly knew who I was and now I am going to be the final decision on who will risk their lives."

"Nobody has to participate. You are just deciding what you want to do. Our group is just trying to assess who is willing and determined. Do not worry. As for who you are," he came over to me, brushed my hair behind my ear, kissed my cheek, and whispered in my ear "You are the girl of my dreams" and then he took my hand and we walk back towards the village.

This was not really the answer I was looking for. It didn't really answer anything. It was another one of those answers that just brought on more questions.

The morning came bringing new light. I stayed up most of the night thinking. About who I am, who I was, and who I want to be. In this I decided, I want to rid myself of the darker parts of my personality that I had in the outside world. Even those who are less pleasant here are worth protecting. I want to keep my determination, my will to survive, and my ability to overcome. As far as who I am, I do not see why this won't improve what I have to work with. I have power, I am learning skill and control, and here I have friends and family, and maybe even my first love. That was one of the few things I still haven't figured out yet. I tried to think about how I feel towards Kethael versus how he feels towards me. The kiss yesterday was somehow proof that I do care for him in some way, but is it enough? That one thought took me longer to try to work out than any other and I was still unsure. For who I want to be, I won't condemn people to death or imprisonment. I will not make decisions for anyone. I spent so much of my life basing my actions and decisions around everyone else. My actions were almost always reaction not initiative. I will not make anyone follow me; I will do what I can to aid others in what they decide to the best of my abilities. It isn't exactly who I am, but it's a direction to move towards. And I have made my decision.

A knock on my door and the sound of commotion outside gets me up and about. I quickly clean myself up, get dressed, and answer the door. The person waiting for me is the last I expect.

The fire elemental, Nimiat.

"I heard about the little meeting you had last night, and then why we are having the meeting today. I wanted to talk to you on the way, if you don't mind?"

"Okay?" I was very confused. Nimiat has never been one of my favorite people here in the garden. He has always been a little crude and openly hostile, even when he was trying to give me praise during training.

"It will be to the point as I am sure you have come to expect from me" I nodded so he continued. "I heard the foretelling long before you came here. Most of us in the garden did. With the foretelling came something else, something I am sure you have taken for granted, it brought hope. Although we strive here in the garden, we bicker amongst ourselves; we complain about what we do to give back to Arhea, we still lacked hope. We care about each other much like a family. When we fight we usually make amends somehow in most cases. Some of the creatures make the exception not the rule." I was confused to what his point is when he adds "This includes you." I stopped dead in my tracks. He looked at me with a superior smirk on his face. "You are like the adopted sibling that a few never really wanted in the first place but you have seemed to worm your way in without realizing it. You are talented and humble at the same time. You are someone worth having in anyone's life. You are worth following and protecting. Keep this in mind when you give your decision." He turned to leave without waiting for a response from me.

This put a new meaning to who I am going to be. Humble is a word I have never applied to myself. I don't think I am humble really. It's more that people see more of me than there really is. But maybe there is more to me and I am the one who can't see it. That doesn't really count as humble either, that would be a lack of confidence. If the people here want me, or have at least accepted me in a way they don't show then maybe I could be what they want. I could try and put all my efforts in whatever their hopes are. I don't want to take that away from them.

I was in a daze as I walked towards the meeting place. I didn't even realize at first that everyone was there waiting for me. All of them; not just the leaders of each group. And all of their eyes were on me as I walked up to Arhea. She leaned down to meet with me as privately as possible. "I will let you do the honors of this meeting, with it give yours and Kethael's answer.

I walked to the center of the crowd, looked around, and made my final decisions. Taking in the looks on everyone's face resolved my feelings of fear and confirmed Nimiat's explanation. I see hope.

"We have an ultimatum at hand. The other side is going to fight no matter what we do. We can become prisoners and watch the outside world crumble and die or we can fight until we ensure nobody left on the other side will try to destroy anymore life whether it is here or out there. I have made my decision. I do not wish anyone to follow or expect outside help. Anyone who chooses to come with me will be welcomed. I am going to fight, to protect them, you, and anyone else who may find their way into the world in the future." I say in a loud clear voice.

Everything stayed quiet, people stop to digest what I said, to make a decision. They look to one another then back to me. In unison they all say in loud, steady, and decided voices

"We Fight!"

I felt like I had been given a jolt of hope myself. If they are all willingly with me then maybe we could do this easily. I still have a nagging in the back of my head, *there are casualties in wars!* but I will do my best to ignore it for now. I will deal with that when the time comes.

Epilogue

After the meeting everything seemed to flow into a pattern. Emerenta spent plenty of time around my home, helping me adjust as much as possible to my new life and responsibility. The friendship from here was one of the elite team relationships that came easily. I could admit things that I worried about with her easily and she would help.

Arhea left me to focus on studies on my own . . . If I had a question I could go to her but she encouraged me to find my own way. Since it seemed that I was becoming a leader of sorts, she wanted me to feel empowered.

Baellon and Zula kept about the same amount of interaction. Zula was cynical and at times bitter but still she pushed me to be the best I could. Baellon was more than a protector, he was a friend. And although his humor was dry at times he still made me smile.

My relationship with Kynis was still strained but it was nice to have a father figure I could depend on.

Jarita had made contact a few times, to offer support. She still seemed like she preferred her cavern.

Kethael however, well to be honest I avoided him as much as possible. After the thoughtless, emotion filled kiss I wasn't sure what to do. I didn't want to feel pressured to be with him but felt like if I ignored the seer I would regret it. It is something I will have to address later.

Most importantly I have focused on my training and prepping for the coming battle and adjusting to life in the garden.

Made in the USA
San Bernardino, CA
28 October 2015